BOOKS BY V.G.KUM

Biography

Gowri

Fiction

Stalking Crime

Non-fiction

Chemistry & Technology of Silicon and Tin

Main Group Elements & Their Compounds

Tin: An under-exploited Resource in National Wealth Creation

Tin in Applications: Meeting the Green Challenge

The Tapestry of Science: A multidisciplinary review of fundamental and contemporary topics

To: Prof. Mohd. Keshavjee

MISSION SABAH

- The Manhunt -

V.G. KUMAR DAS

'Orangutan and its young'
(Photo credit: Thomas Fuhrmann, CC BY-SA 4.0, via Wikipedia Commons)

With warmest best wishes,

VG Kumar Das

COPYRIGHT

DISCLAIMER

This is a fictional narrative set in the Malaysian state of Sabah. Consequently, it carries a description of the state's geography, including names of some of its towns and villages, and a few reflections on its authentic history. However, all other names, characters, organizations, locales, events, and incidents cited in the story are solely the product of the author's imagination or are used fictitiously. The book is in no way meant to hurt the sensitivities of any individual, race or religion. Any resemblance to actual persons, living or dead, is entirely coincidental.

DEDICATION

This book is dedicated, with love and affection, to my wife, Datin Dr Ambikadevi. Her persuasiveness is responsible for introducing me to the thrills and joy of writing books beyond the technical realm. The book equally is dedicated to my children and grandchildren who have imbibed the reading habit and enjoy a good yarn.

ACKNOWLEDGEMENTS

My grateful thanks go to my dear friends, Kumar Menon and Pushpa Menon, and my sister, Valsala Panicker, for their critical reading of original drafts of the manuscript which has helped me immensely to improve the overall presentation of the narrative. My thanks also go to my daughter, Dr Gouri, for meticulously editing the manuscript and assembling it for publication in the Amazon Kindle format.

PROLOGUE:

The story unfolds with the arrival of the antagonist – the much-feared jihadist terrorist, Saadam Elwan - in East Malaysia some four months before the country's Ministry of Defence (MinDef) gets wind of his presence that forebode a serious threat to the nation's security. Knee-jerked into action, MinDef picks its top counter-terrorism agent, ASP Zainal Abidin ("Zain") to head a 7-member elite task force on a manhunt for the adversary and smother the network of clandestine terror cells being created.

CHAPTER 1

$\mathcal{T}$he ship, *Rongyu*, that docked at the mist-shrouded port of Karachi late that evening in August was a gearless container. It had sailed in from Shanghai. In its hold was all the equipment required for the new railway line that China was building from Karachi to Peshawar, a distance of over 1,000 kilometres.

Sheikh Gafoor Khan, anxiously pacing up and down the floor of his house, greeted the news of the ship's arrival with a sigh of relief. He was the principal logistics man behind the 2008 Mumbai terror attack by the radicalised group Lashkar-e-Taiba. Hiding from the police and the ever-lurking eyes of the Indian Intelligence Agency, RAW, he had sneaked in from Azad Kashmir to a run-down, single-storey house located in Kiamari, near Karachi. He had been charged months earlier by the Lashkar-e-Taiba High Command to covertly despatch three jihadists to the Philippines "undetected by enemies of Islam".

Information about them was carried by hand to him by a chain of couriers, the last one of whom he was asked to meet at the home of a skilled underground passport forger in the town of Hyderabad, some three hours' drive from Karachi. He hadn't personally met any of them before, and he was particularly looking forward to meeting one among them, a top-ranking member of the jihadist group Islamic State (IS), also known as ISIS. His name: Saadam Elwan.

The other two jihadists accompanying Saadam, he was told, were from the Mindanao-based Bangsamoro Islamic Freedom Fighters; they were serving as Saadam's bodyguards, having completed their training in Syria. They were all coming for the meeting from the mountainous Taliban stronghold in the Bajajur district in northern Pakistan that shares its border with Afghanistan.

Sheikh Gafoor knew what to expect from the meeting. Earlier that day, he had met the *hawala* man in downtown Karachi, who had handed him in exchange for a promissory note two bagsful of USD 100 bills. He had a lot of people to take care of at the port before the ship headed back to Shanghai. Much of his time, he knew, would be taken up tomorrow in arranging for his visitors to board the ship unnoticed while he had to deal with the 'helpers' on the ground, keeping his own identity intact.

It was close to midnight when the visitors finally arrived. The sheikh greeted each of them at the door with a tight hug and three cheek-to-cheek embraces, and the equally traditional Arabic greeting, *"Assalamu alaikum."* He offered them refreshments while outlining to them the plan for transporting them to Southeast Asia aboard the Chinese container ship.

"You will board the ship with forged identification as Pakistani agents of the Ishtha shipping group, and I have arranged to take you past security and customs without a hitch. Our people will come here to fetch you in a police vehicle. The ship will set to sail around 3.00 p.m. tomorrow. You will be picked up by a fishing boat when the ship veers close to Basilan, an island province of the Philippines in the South China Sea, from where you will go by car or ferry to Zamboanga city. There's a regular ferry from Zamboanga to Sandakan in Sabah that you can take, provided your cover is not blown," said a confident Sheikh, looking at the nodding bodyguards. They appeared to have understand a smattering of the conversation wholly in Arabic.

"You have gone to great lengths to arrange this. We are grateful," said a beaming Saadam.

"My pleasure, *sayidi* (sir). I noted your destination was Sabah, but I'm in the dark about your trip," ventured the sheikh, not sure whether his inquisitiveness would be welcomed.

Saadam gave him a searching look before replying, "Political Islam is gaining ground in Southeast Asia, which is home to a large proportion of the global Muslim population. A large part of Sabah in Malaysia was once an Islamic Sulu State. The Muslims there, along with their brethren in the southern Philippines, are calling for the establishment of an Islamic State in that part of the world." The words were in Arabic. Switching next to English, he continued:

"We salute our Bangsamoro Islamic Freedom Fighters in their effort towards realising this. My role will be to assist them in their organisational effort. I hope you understand that no one should get wind of my mission. The utmost secrecy must prevail."

"Most assuredly, sayidi," responded the Sheikh, also in English. Next, handing Saadam one of the bags in his possession, he whispered to him in Arabic, "And for the cash that you had sought, sayidi, you will find the full amount in denominations of USD 100 in this bag." The sheikh then bid his leave to retire for the night.

Saadam's entry into Sandakan from Zamboanga was some four weeks after sailing from Karachi. He was with an elderly group of returning Haj pilgrims with Philippine passports who had been residing in Sabah since the 1970s. He stood out as an Imam among them. The immigration officials, given to the religious sentiment of returning pilgrims, allowed them through.

Saadam was immediately taken away in a waiting car to a house in an oil palm plantation on the outskirts of Sandakan town. This was considered a secure enough place, away from the prying eyes of security forces. He had with him his two same bodyguards. They were taken to an end house with a small side garden that was part of a terraced lot of four single-storey houses. Their immediate neighbour was Haji Jalah, the man who had fetched them at the jetty. He told them that he was their 'assigned' caretaker.

Jalah was a harvesting *mandore* entrusted with overseeing the collection of ripe palm fruit bunches from the trees. Almost fifty percent of the field workers in the plantation under his watch were foreigners recruited from the Philippines and Indonesia; the rest were illegals from the archipelagos of Sulu and Tawi-Tawi or from mainland Mindanao who had come by speedboat and landed at remote coastal towns of the state. Saadam couldn't have wished for a better pool of potential recruits to be placed in his lap, but he knew he had to be cautious – all the more so until he was sure of the credentials of his assigned caretaker who had been thrust on him.

Jalah spoke only Malay and some broken English, but he understood some elementary Arabic. Over the course of a week, Saadam learnt that Jalah had performed his haj some four years back and that one of his sons who had got a scholarship from the educational wing of an indigenous Pribumi political party to pursue Islamic studies in Egypt had suddenly dropped his studies midstream to help the jihadists in Syria. The information was music to Saadam's ears, but he was determined not to blow his cover.

Reminiscing about his safe journey into Sabah, he appreciated the quiet efficiency of the Bangsamoro Islamic Freedom Fighters. He had met one of their leaders at Basilan Island, who had assured him that he would be contacted by their supporters once he reached Sandakan.

He soon got up to speed with the prevailing politics in the state, the security net that the Sabah Coastline Security Command (SCSC) had woven around the land, and importantly, from his perspective, the brewing disgruntlement among the large number of stateless citizens who were unable to fend for the educational and healthcare needs of their children. The more he thought about the plight of these hapless non-citizens, the more convinced he was that one of the routes to fulfilling the Islamic State's goal in the region was through the establishment of madrasas in mosques (masjid) or prayer halls (surau) in remote plantations and villages. He would then have the right cadre of people nurtured for the cause, with a multiplier effect when a fatwa calling for the restoration of an Islamic Sulu State is made. He discreetly enquired of Jalah whether there was a nearby masjid or a surau where he could create a free educational centre for children deprived of the opportunity to attend public schools. Jalah was excited at the prospect and offered to help him to organise the effort and even seek supporting funds from the plantation management.

11

"That may not be necessary just yet. Let me think it over. Our chances of getting funds will be better once we have made a start," asserted Saadam with a confident voice.

"No masjid here, tuan (sir), but have *dewan masyarakat* (community hall). Can use it as a surau. No problem." responded Jalah.

"That's excellent," replied Saadam.

At mid-afternoon a couple of days later, a truck drove up to Saadam's hideout. The visitors were a group of two locals and a foreigner. One of the locals stepped forward towards Saadam and introduced himself as Dr Amiruddin Mohamed. He added that he was a university lecturer specialising in agronomics and was attached to the Sandakan branch campus of a local university. He then introduced the foreigner, Imran Mehmed, a Bosnian refugee who had escaped the 1992–1995 Bosnian War and was now settled in Sabah; and finally, the other local, Idris Mohamed, who was an influential member of a Pribumi party in the state.

"He also happens to be my brother," remarked the lecturer.

"How did you know about this place?" asked a somewhat surprised Saadam.

"I was instrumental in locating you here. We had been alerted about your impending arrival several months back, and we're here to offer you every assistance that you may require," answered Amiruddin.

"Is it safe to move around?"

"In disguise and by avoiding the highways. Haji Jalah is an entrusted member of our group. He knows all the small roads and river routes around here."

Saadam turned to look towards Jalah and gave an understanding nod.

"How are you in all this?" This time the question was directed by Saadam to the Bosnian.

"I have the connections to getting the hardware that you would need. I parade as an undercover agent for the police. This helps me to run my errands through runners I pretend I'm after. Only on one instance did the police beat me to them while I was in a pretend chase, but the runners were killed in the gun battle that followed."

"I'm not sure I understand you. What's the hardware you are talking about?"

"I mean guns, explosives, and detonators, and also materials for making improvised explosive devices (IEDs)," answered the Bosnian.

"Where do you get them, and for whom are you buying and transporting these?"

"For more than a year I have been having close deals first with the Abu Sayaff and then with the Bangsamoro group. You know there is a big crackdown on gun manufacturing in the Philippines. Many gunsmiths have come over here and are involved in their clandestine manufacture, mostly around Tawau. I have the means to transport the firearms procured from overseas and those made here by speedboats to a few island destinations on our east coast. And I have successfully done so by evading the coastal guards."

There was an appreciative smile on Saadam's face, but he wasn't finished yet. "So, you handle both the procurement and delivery?"

"Mostly the delivery. I have a compatriot who helps with just the overseas procurement."

"Hmm! I take it you're not just a mere businessman, but one who is committed to our cause here in this region?"

"Wholeheartedly, sir. My suffering in Bosnia is enough to last a lifetime. Our faith there lacked the resilience and militant vigour I find with you all."

Saadam gave him a long look before next asking, "And how did you come in contact with the brothers here?"

"By chance. I met Dr Amiruddin at a pro-Bosnia rally in Kuala Lumpur, and we have been friends since."

Satisfied, Saadam turned to Idris. "Are all your party members in sync with the establishment of an Islamic State?"

"No, only a small fraction is leaning towards that goal. But a strong rally led by us would be well received by the majority of the population. The shift will be full once the local government is rattled and the public sentiment is sufficiently aroused towards an Islamic rather than a secular state by your efforts here."

Saadam cleared his throat and settled back in his chair, with his eyes momentarily closed and his palms clasped together, with the tips of his fingers caressing his nose. He then opened his eyes and said in a pedagogical voice, "We can only succeed, and succeed we will if we approach this from two angles." There was rapt attention as he continued. "You have heard of soft power, haven't you? That's putting the delights of pure Islam as embodied in the Holy Koran in front of the population who have been fed on falsehoods and Western cultural decadence. But soft power alone will not work. It has to be strengthened and sustained by hard power – the jihad to fight the kafirs by whatever means, even if it entails forsaking our own lives for the cause of Islam." He paused to gulp in some water from a glass that the obsequious Haji Jalah handed him before continuing.

"I feel that we can win over the confidence and trust of a large number of hapless non-citizens in the state who struggle for their livelihood by giving them and their children informal Islamic education free in madrasahs that we can establish in villages and plantations such as this. Over time, we can build a cadre of people bent to our cause whom we can place in several madrasahs to gain a quick turnaround. Haji Jalah has said a start could be made here using the community hall. We need teachers and funding, of course, to get a head start here before duplicating the effort elsewhere."

"That's a marvellous idea. I'm sure our party's educational arm can provide some funds that you might need," observed Idris.

"I agree," echoed his brother. "Leave it to me to source some retired teachers who can help you on this. But your operation here must not surface. This means the suggestion to the plantation management for the use of the community hall must come from others employed here, including a couple of Muslim management staff. I'm sure Haji Jalah can look into this."

"Yes, I shall. Perhaps the plantation management might even agree to give a matching grant to what the Pribumi party may condescend to offer," chuckled Saadam.

"Do you have some basic curriculum in mind?" asked Amiruddin.

"Yes, of course. I have previously been a teacher. It will be conducted in two phases. Phase one of the studies will be for students of all age groups to teach them the basics of the Arabic language so that they can better understand our Islamic Beliefs and learn to memorise and recite the verses in the Holy Koran. The classes could be from 9.00 a.m. to noon for children, and from 4.00 p.m. to 7.00 p.m. for male adults, spread over four days a week, excluding Fridays. I'm sure you can help get some local teachers for this phase. For the subsequent phase two of the programme, or simultaneously for those with a smattering knowledge of Arabic, I shall personally handle that in the confines of this house or a nearby surau thrice a week, if that can be discreetly arranged," responded Saadam, with no further elaboration.

"How sure are you of getting students for this religious instruction?" asked Imran.

"Muslims all over the world are afraid of being told that they do not know about their religion. So, they will come. Also, you have many here, I'm told, who habitually speak Malay, and carry Muslim names, but have no full understanding of Islam."

"Hmm," mused Imran. "But what about the hard power training bit?"

"The training with weapons in hand will have to be conducted secretly for selected students of the second phase at the end of their induction period, and also for other recruits brought in by our field agents. The training, of course, has to be in camps that are being created by BIFF. Their scouts are already on the field. However, on an urgent basis, I want you to secure two sets of revolvers and ammunition for my bodyguards here, and also the ingredients that I have compiled in this list for an IED," came the prompt reply from Saadam, handing the Bosnian the list from his notebook. The meeting then dispersed, with Saadam agreeing to meet them again in a fortnight.

It took around three months before Saadam's idea of the madrasah could come to fruition, with an initial enrolment of around forty students. The cost of mobile whiteboards, a few side screens, mobile partitions and carpets, Wi-Fi installation, and some minor non-permanent modifications at the community hall was borne by Saadam himself. Donations in the form of a photostat machine, three computers, fifty school bags with notebooks and pencils, and fifty copies of the Holy Koran, were received from well-wishers and unwittingly through the educational arm of the Pribumi party. Amiruddin successfully solicited two part-time teaching staff for the madrasah through his contacts with state-run religious schools and local mosques.

Saadam was pleased with the efforts. He was careful, however, to keep a low profile, and settled on a regular disguise whenever he left his dwelling or met his guests there. Saadam made only infrequent visits to the madrasah, and at its soft launch which was only attended by plantation workers, he was introduced to them as one of its benefactors-cum-advisor. But unknown to others, while work was in progress on the madrasah, he had used a carpenter from the pool of hired personnel to partition a room in his dwelling to create a secret room with soundproof walls. Access to this room was through a pull-out bookshelf, known only to himself and his bodyguards, besides the carpenter. This room, he decided, was going to be his temporary laboratory where he would indulge in the fabrication of IED. The carpenter was handsomely rewarded for his job, but his lips were permanently sealed soon thereafter by one of the bodyguards in a staged accident.

CHAPTER 2

*I*nspector Zainal Abidin ("Zain") opened the sealed envelope that Datuk Azhari Yakub, the high-ranking civil service official at the Malaysian Ministry of Defence (MinDef), handed him across the table. A broad smile spread across his face as he read the contents.

"It says here that I have been promoted to assistant superintendent of police (ASP), and am being attached to the National Special Operations Force at the Ministry of Defence."

"The promotion is well-deserved, and your posting was a joint decision by both the Ministry of Home Affairs and MinDef. When do you officially report for duty?"

"As per the letter, on the first of December - about two weeks from now."

"Good. Take a small break, but remember to come in tomorrow morning for the joint forces command briefing. The commander, General Ghazali Abu Hassan, sounded somewhat agitated when he spoke to me about the briefing a couple of days back, but he specifically wanted me to contact and bring you to the security briefing."

"Yes, sir, I shall be there; but I wonder why?"

"No doubt it has a lot to do with how well you handled your recent solo mission. Something tells me that you are being roped in for a higher-level engagement." Walking back to his car, Zain reminisced on the successful solo mission that had towards the end nearly snatched him into the jaws of death. He felt a little shudder in his body, but his strong-willed mind drew him back to the faceless enemies of the nation that still hounded him. They lurked everywhere. He had only succeeded, he knew, in netting a few. And he wondered about the meeting to which he was again being summoned at MinDef, this time by General Ghazali. Was fate drawing him again to new encounters with the enemy? He was not to know this yet, but the scene was already set in faraway Karachi some six months earlier for unleashing unprecedented terror into the country.

The next morning, summoned by habit, Zain's eyes blinked open at the same time as the grandfather clock in the hallway of his house chimed five times. Getting out of bed, he drew back the curtain at the window. The sky was still pitch dark. Dawn was yet to break. The only light that caught his eyes was the distant intermittent flashes of lightning that occasionally came together in a furious instant to create a jagged streak of intense white light to rip the night sky. He opened the window and inhaled deeply. The air was cold and refreshing, and it carried the earthy aroma of approaching rain that Zain quite welcomed.

He moved away as soon as he heard a mild groan from his 4-year old daughter Zaleha who was deep in slumber. He bent over her and gently kissed her forehead, not wanting to wake her up or disturb his wife Mariam who was at her side, fast asleep. Zain then went about his morning routine, getting himself ready for the meeting with Datuk Azhari Yaakub at the Ministry of Defence (Mindef). The meeting had been scheduled for 8.30 am, and with time on his hands, Zain decided to have his breakfast outside at his favourite restaurant that overlooked the traffic lights at the junction of the roads, Jalan Tun Razak and Jalan Semarak. To him, the breakfast menu of *nasi lemak* (fragrant rice dish cooked in coconut milk and pandan leaf) and *teh tarik* (literally 'pulled tea') served at the restaurant was unmatched elsewhere in the city of Kuala Lumpur, and MinDef was conveniently just some 3 km away from the restaurant off Jalan Semarak.

Arriving at the restaurant which was on the first floor of the building, he found himself a seat that gave him a vantage view of the junction. There were few cars at that hour on the roads, and Zain watched with envy the lights at the junction switching from red to green at a faster pace than he had ever experienced. He had always groaned at the delay at the junction whenever he had to cross it. Casually looking at the junction while tucking into his nasi lemak, his eyes caught a black Mercedes with an army number plate arriving at the junction to turn into Jalan Semarak. There was only a red Proton Exora ahead of it. Suddenly, out of nowhere, he saw a motorcycle roar up alongside both cars. The rider halted to allow his pillion passenger who was brandishing a gun to fire several shots into the Mercedes, and slip in a parcel under the vehicle before the duo sped away. That the parcel contained an improvised explosive device was soon clear, as within moments a loud explosion ripped through the car.

Watching the scene in utter disbelief, Zain felt the agonising experience he had recently lived through creeping upon him. With adrenaline flying through him, he sprinted down the stairs, leapt over the road barrier, and ran towards the Mercedes. A couple of others immediately joined him to prise open the doors of the burning car and bring out its two dead occupants to the road's edge along Jalan Semarak.

There was pandemonium all around. Cars came to a screeching halt at the roads, all curious to know what had happened at the traffic junction. A couple of occupants who were in the back seats of the Proton Exora and a few pedestrians sustained injuries on account of the explosion which had flung dangerous projectiles of metal and glass fragments into the surroundings. They were all guided away to a safe place. Sensing the rising intensity of flames enveloping the car, and a possible explosion that may arise from the car's fuel tank, Zain loudly waived everyone off who was approaching the scene, uttering *"Undur Undur! Mungkin ada letupan lagi!"* (Back off! Back off! Another explosion is likely!). He had himself barely reached the road's edge when the petrol tank exploded, knocking off the traffic lights and claiming more victims on the road.

Soon, the sounds of a fire engine and an ambulance filled the air. Zain moved away upon their arrival on the scene. He surmised that the non-driver who was killed was a high-ranking army officer. The badges that were pinned on his uniform attested to that. To Zain, the dastardly act didn't quite fit the bill of conventional gangster warfare. Datuk Azhari, he was sure, would have the handle on it. Reaching for his mobile phone, he called Azhari and narrated the event that had taken place.

Oh, my God! That must have been Colonel Nik Ismail, the commander of our security forces in Sabah and Sarawak. Stay put where you are. Don't use your car. I shall send a military police jeep to fetch you.

Zain was greeted at the entrance to MinDef with a warm embrace from a hugely relieved Azhari. "*Alhamdulilah* (Praise be to God) your car was not on the spot as well. You could have been an unintended victim."

Zain trembled thinking about the incident that Azhari had alluded to. He was lucky to have survived a similar bomb blast in his car at the tail end of his last mission. If not for the fly in his car that had caused him to ill-position himself on the seat while shooing it off through the still open door, he would have been blown to smithereens.

"We're shocked and saddened that Colonel Nik Ismail had met his fate at the hands of assassins. Anti-national elements must be behind this, working in collusion with foreigners," said Azhari, without further elaboration, and deep in thought.

Ushering Zain to his office, Azhari went up to his desk to order some coffee. He looked visibly disturbed.

"Who were Colonel Nik Ismail's killers? What was their aim? How did they know he was heading here for a meeting?" He felt uneasy as the questions whirled in his mind, even more so at the thought that his establishment could be harbouring spies.

Finishing their coffee in silence, both of them then left to attend the meeting on one of the building's top floors, accessible for security reasons, only on a private elevator with private access. Zain found the officers of the joint command were all in their seats ahead of time. He spotted the Secretary to MinDef, the inspector general of police, and the Senior Assistant Commissioner of Police Mokhtar, all of whom were seated among the front rows. Zain earned a nod of recognition and a smile from Mokhtar, whom he had last seen when Zain was being treated in hospital for reconstructive facial surgery after escaping the bomb blast in his car.

General Ghazali entered the briefing room punctually on the hour, bringing everyone to their feet. He went straight to ASP Zain to shake his hands and have a word with him before proceeding to the lectern.

"*Assalamu alaikum.* Good morning everyone; please be seated. Ladies and gentlemen, I have called this meeting to convey to you all some grave news about Sabah. But before I come to that, I have to break the sad news that Colonel Nik Ismail, who is overall in charge of our security forces in East Malaysia, was killed by unknown assassins as he was making his way here to the meeting."

Anger and anguish greeted the announcement. Several people, uncharacteristic of military personnel, got up distraught, fielding a barrage of questions, all wanting to know more.

Waiving them back to their seats, the General continued. "Colonel Nik and his driver were both shot dead by unknown gunmen on a motorbike as his car halted at the lights at the junction of Jalan Semarak and Jalan Tun Razak. The colonel was a brave and exceptional soldier who had seen service with the United Nations peacekeeping force. He was also an extraordinary military strategist and we had pinned our hopes on him in tightening our security measures in Sabah. We shall mourn his loss and shall leave no stone unturned to find the scoundrels and their masterminds responsible for his death. Let's observe a minute's silence; *Al-Faatihah.*

Thank you, ladies and gentlemen. Now for the grave news about Sabah. According to the CIA alert that we received barely 48 hours ago, a top-ranking member of the jihadist group Islamic State or ISIS had been dispatched to our region some months ago. His name is Saadam Elwan. Indications are that he is headed towards Sabah; perhaps he's already there. The audacious fatal attack on Colonel Nik is certainly linked to this security threat that is unfolding in Sabah."

The audience this time sat in stunned silence at the news. Fear and anger were very palpable in the room as General Ghazali continued, "ISIS has also aligned with the Bangsamoro Islamic Freedom Fighters from the Philippines in pursuit of their activities to propagate radicalised Islam. The Bangsamoro as you all know, has been championing the Islamic Sulu claims to parts of eastern Sabah, and their incursions continue along the state's eastern coast. Not to mention also the sporadic kidnapping for ransom attacks by notorious elements of Abu Sayaff, another Filipino Islamist guerrilla group. Our security concerns here are, therefore, very real as the entire stretch of the coastline is some 1,700 kilometres long."

As he said so, he tapped a keyboard recessed in the well of the lectern. A large map of Sabah popped up on the giant flat TV monitor on the wall behind him. The lights in the room automatically dimmed and the blinds slid over the windows to further brighten the monitor.

Turning toward the TV monitor, he continued, "As you can see here, the state has two major Divisions on its eastern seaboard – Sandakan, facing the Sulu Sea, and Tawau, facing the Celebes Sea in the south. Both these

27

divisions have witnessed sporadic acts of militancy, pirating, kidnapping, and sabotage over the years. However, of late, such acts have greatly intensified and appear well-coordinated, as if there is an unseen hand behind them. Intelligence reports reaching us have revealed that there is an underground plot to bring down the state government. Insurgents have penetrated some key government agencies where cybersecurity appears to be abysmally low or virtually absent. The rumour is widespread that a 'shadow government' is already in place, awaiting a return of the Sulu sultanate that was in existence there between the seventeenth and eighteenth centuries. The claim is that each day, they are gaining new adherents from various parts of Borneo Island, the Bangsamoro Islamic Freedom Fighters among them."

"Can you shed more light on who is behind the Sulu sultanate claim?" asked someone from the audience.

"There is a self-proclaimed Sulu Sultan Jamalul Kiram III, based in Manila, who is staking the claim for the return from the Malaysian government of the territorial areas in Sabah that are considered the sacred land of the Tausug or Suluk peoples. In February 2013 he took the bold but abortive step of occupying Kampung Tanduo, a small village at Tanjung Labian, about 100 kilometres from Lahad Datu, with his Royal Sulu Force of 200 militants originating from the island chain of Tawi-Tawi in the southern Philippines. One of his demands to our government, besides acknowledging his rights to the claim, was that his group be paid compensation amounting to USD 7.5 billion for occupying Sabah since 1963.

He paused to continue. "Following this unexpected attack, which was repelled, the government wasted no time in tightening up the security in the state, particularly along its east coast. A security committee that came to be known as the Sabah Coastline Security Command, or SCSC for short, was established, headquartered in Lahad Datu. Seven areas on the eastern seaboard, as shown here on this map, namely, Kudat-Pitas, Beluran, Sandakan, Kinabatangan, Lahad Datu, Tawau, and Kunak-Semporna, were identified by SCSC as being particularly vulnerable to attack by intruders. We have beefed up security at key points in these places which are collectively known as the Coastal Area Security Hubs, or CASH for short. The security concern, as I said, is very grave. To be precise, we have 1,733 kilometres of coastline, and an area of 31,158 square kilometres with 362 islands to guard against intruders."

"Don't we have the army there now well marshalled against any future attacks?" asked another voice from the audience.

"We don't have an army camp presently on the east coast on the scale of the two camps that we have at Lok Kawi and Kota Belud in the West Coast Division. Here, you can see their locations on the map." A zoom-in view of the West Coast Division appeared on the monitor, and the general used his laser pointer to trace a line between the two red spots on the screen where the camps were located.

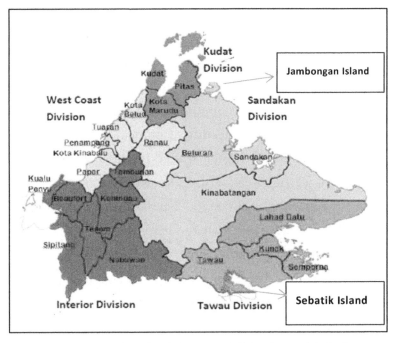

Map showing Divisions and Districts of Sabah

(Source: William, T, Rahman, HA & Barber, B 2013,

PLoS Neglected Tropical Diseases, vol. 7, no. 1, e2026)

Wearing a worried expression, he continued. "And there have been unconfirmed reports of sabotage of several army vehicles in these camps. We are presently keeping the news under wraps.

"Have we not deployed maritime patrol aircraft and drones in the hunt for the saboteurs?" asked an officer who was in naval uniform.

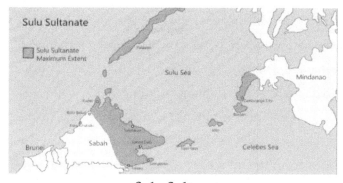

Sulu Sultanate

Source:http://www.mkenology.com/2013/03/the-sulu-sultanate-and sabah.html

"Yes, we have deployed them, but we don't have enough of them to comb the vast area. SCSC has asked for more aerial support, but their request remains unfulfilled. The commander of SCSC is here with us, and you will have a chance to hear more from him later on about the strategic measures being taken to counter the security threat. These have included the imposition of dusk-to-dawn sea curfews covering areas up to three nautical miles off Tawau, Semporna, Kunak, Lahad Datu, Kinabatangan, Sandakan, and Beluran."

"I would have thought that with the creation of SCSC, one or two army bases would have been established in the CASH areas such as at Sandakan or Tawau by now," opined SAC Mokhtar.

Nodding, General Ghazali replied, "That was also our expectation. However, I understand MinDef is still mulling over our request, as it costs hundreds of millions ringgits to establish an army base to house a regiment of several battalions. It is, however, no secret that SCSC has set up small army camps in Sandakan, at the mouth of the Kinabatangan River, Semporna, Kunak, and Tawau." Lighted green spots suddenly appeared on the map, giving their locations. "CASH," continued Ghazali, "actually operates from its military garrison at Lahad Datu."

"How about naval or air bases on the east coast?" Mokhtar pressed.

"We have a naval base at Sandakan, but in Tawau we still operate from a base off the Kunak coast. This is essentially a decommissioned oil rig retrofitted into a permanent sea base. As you might know, the Royal Malaysian Navy has been entrusted to enforce CASH. There are no air force bases *per se*, only air operation support centres presently at the airports in Sandakan and Tawau; the principal Royal Malaysian Air Force (RMAF) base is still at Labuan".

"What moves are you now contemplating, sir, concerning the present crisis?" asked one of the senior officers.

"I'm coming to that," said General Ghazali. Worry rippled his voice. "If Saadam is anywhere in Sabah, we need to apprehend him and break up the network he might have already created. If possible, we need to capture him alive. His mission is clear – to set up as many terror cells as possible, and organise militancy on a scale perhaps larger and more ominous than we have witnessed during our

Emergency years fighting Communist insurgency. If you ask me, we have to deal stealth with stealth. We need to despatch undercover operatives on the field in Sabah who can also effectively execute commando-style operations, where necessary, with the full knowledge of SCSC."

Then, turning towards Zain with a smile unfolding across his face, he beckoned Zain to stand up.

"Ladies and gentlemen, let me introduce you to ASP Zainal - our first-hand witness at the killing of Colonel Nik Ismail this morning. He will assist us in our probe in more ways than one. Some of you here perhaps already know that he had accomplished an amazing undercover job while capturing the culprits of the banned Al-Ma'unah Islamic terrorist group responsible for the bombing at our Merdeka Day parade last year. He has also stalked and apprehended other saboteurs and high-end criminals, risking his life. Indeed, he miraculously escaped a car bomb attempt on his life while on his previous assignment. I have invited him here because we have a special role for him in the new security measures we're planning for Sabah. He is the kind of pahlawan (warrior) we need for the special intelligence commando group I mentioned. I hope ASP Zainal will agree to lead this elite force we intend to set up immediately."

"My life is for my country's asking," replied Zain to loud cheers from the audience.

"The force will initially comprise of two groups of three members each, who will be given an intense two months of training at the Terendak military camp in Melaka. Each group will have a commanding officer, and the overall Sabah operations of these groups will be led by ASP Zainal, who shall attach himself to any group where his presence may be deemed necessary. One group will be deployed in Sandakan and the other in Tawau. Each group will carefully recruit others from the state to be their eyes and ears on the ground – you might want to call them 'shadow recruits'. Selected members among them will be sent for training in the military camp in Kota Belud for potential appointment as members of the Peoples' Voluntary Corps (RELA). The details have to be worked out. The groups will be required to report all their findings of clandestine activities in the state that potentially impinge on security to SCSC, who will keep us in the loop. This also includes any commando raids they might contemplate on identified targets.

"The commander of SCSC, Deputy Commissioner of Police Datuk Johari Sulaiman, will now address you. He will be followed by my deputy who will touch on some aspects of our overall military logistics in that state."

The whole session lasted about an hour and a half, at the end of which Zain followed Azhari back to his office to gather some additional pointers on the geography and varied ethnicity of the peoples of Sabah.

CHAPTER 3

*T*he training stint at the military camp at Terendak was delayed by a week to allow Zain to obtain full health clearance from his doctors. The bomb blast that he miraculously survived at the end of his last mission had necessitated extended medical leave which he had only recently exhausted. But MinDef wasn't taking any chances. They wanted him to be in perfect health and fitness for the arduous task ahead.

Joining him at Terendak, he noted with some pleasure, was Kamal, an ex-colleague of his from the police field force. They had shared many escapades in hunting remnant members of militant groups and armed drug smuggling gangs across the breadth of peninsular Malaysia. They were happy that their experience was recognized and directed toward a national security cause.

Among the other hand-picked recruits by MinDef there were two police officers – Inspectors Samy and Azlan, and three army personnel – Lieutenant Dhanyal and two female officers, Major Sungkiah and Captain Dr. Su Eng. Zain immediately immersed himself in getting to know their personal histories to establish a level of camaraderie that was critical for their mission. Aside from Sungkiah, a Kadazan from Sabah, the remainder were from Peninsular

Malaysia all of whom have had brief stints of service previously in the state during their training or service postings. They were thus no strangers to the land. Zain also knew he could beef up his team, if needed, with local asset recruitment.

It was a gruelling physical training stint that Zain and his comrades had to undergo at Terendak and elsewhere arranged by the instructors at the camp. The training included parachuting, rafting, and wilderness survival, but they all sailed through the training with little hiccups. Lessons on the strategy and tactics of guerrilla warfare, handling of electronic spyware, and geographical and demographic features of Sabah were also critical parts of their training programme.

Zain helped organise the trainees into two groups, as previously suggested by General Ghazali. He named the groups Pasukan Pahlawan (Warrior Team) PP1 and PP2. Sungkiah, Azlan and Dhanyal were assigned to PP1, while Kamal, Samy and Su Eng made up PP2. Sungkiah and Kamal were appointed the commanding officers of their respective groups. As the mission's leader, Zain would coordinate the efforts of both groups while also participating by attaching himself to either group as demanded by the nature of the operation. The PP1 group, it was decided, would descend on Tawau, while PP2 would cover the Sandakan Division. The discrete presence of the two groups in Sabah was to be intimated by MinDef to only three individuals in the state whose mobile phone numbers were given in strict confidence to Zain. They were: Assistant Commissioner Mohd Arshad, the OCPD at the Sandakan Police Headquarters; Brigadier General Othman Basiron, the director of SCSC's Armed Forces Operational Centre; and Deputy Commissioner of Police Datuk Sulaiman Johari, the commander of SCSC stationed in Lahad Datu. It was made clear to the pahlawans that to protect their covert operations, they would present themselves to any external party as a logistics appraisal team sent by MinDef.

It was on the first Saturday of March that Zain and his pahlawans boarded the Royal Malaysian Airforce plane that took them to Sandakan town, the second largest in Sabah after the west coast city of Kota Kinabalu. Upon arrival, they were all taken on a special police bus to the guesthouse at Villa Permai, discreetly arranged by Arshad. At the guesthouse, they were informed that a studio room for Zain and three twin-bedded rooms for the others had been reserved for their occupancy for four days. The pahlawans carried their luggage to their rooms without being subject to any security screening. The items in their possession included weapons and a range of military surveillance equipment required for their mission.

They were immensely pleased with the features they found at the guesthouse – a fitness centre, an outdoor pool, free Wi-Fi service, and free shuttle service, all of which eminently suited their immediate needs. They also found their rooms were all on the same floor.

The pahlawans were all aware that as their coordinator Zain was entrusted by MinDef to plan and make the necessary arrangements for transport, accommodation, and subsistence for their entire stay in Sabah. They had, in agreeing to join the mission, pledged Zain their full confidence and loyalty in leading them and managing their affairs. As it was their first day together in Sabah, Zain gave them the day off but reminded them to be present the next morning for a meeting in the guesthouse's only function room. He also offered them a piece of advice with a disarmingly bland smile on his lips: "Do not let your guard down. It's best to be reticent when approached by Sabahans. They're a curious lot, I'm told!"

The pahlawans were already seated when Zain entered the meeting room the next morning. He carried with him his laptop and two large maps – one of the Sandakan Division and the other of Tawau. He greeted them all cordially and after some small talk, commenced the proceedings of the meeting.

"Each one of you has been provided with a special encrypted cell phone. You will find the names of everyone in the team except your own listed under 'Favourites' when you depress the phone call icon. We have previously gone through the drill on how to receive messages and make calls on the phone. Suffice to remind you that no outside calls other than among us are to be entertained. Also, I want to draw your attention specifically to the Self-Destructing Message app installed on your phones. This enables you to send a distress audio message as well as to alert the rest of us if your normal calls to any of us go unanswered. The message will be self-erased as per the expiry time that you set for it, say a minute or two. All audio messages will be treated as an alert to a potentially dangerous developing situation. The app allows you also to send text messages, pictures, and videos. The sender's name is never shown on the same screen as the message. Also, the messages are screenshot-proof and untraceable. Is that clear?"

Receiving their nods, Zain continued. "And, one more thing: You were told when given the special dual-SIM phones that you will never get to use the second SIM number. You must have wondered why. The reason is security. Our special cell phones will be a gift if they fell into enemy hands. If caught and you're forced to surrender your phone, all you need to do is to send me an urgent one-word message "Gone 1" from your smart cellular watch which comes with a built-in SIM. I will immediately sense your location and know that you alone have been caught. If the message was 'Gone 2' or 'Gone 3', I will know how many members of your team are in that predicament. My response then will be to make a call to your unused second SIM number on your cell phone. This will automatically trigger a self-destruct signal causing a power surge in your phone battery, and you will see your phone self-destruct in mere seconds."

"Wow! Mission Impossible-style," exclaimed Su Eng. "My smartwatch is extra special - it can if worn on a patient read his blood pressure and track his ECG."

"Really? Amazing how technology has progressed", chipped in Kamal.

"Yes, indeed," agreed Zain. "Be careful also with the use of your video-camera sunglasses. I hope you have not forgotten the instructions you have received at Terendak on their use."

The teams gave Zain the thumbs-up sign. But he had not finished. "Another point I want to make is that no one giving you even a glance should suspect your police or army background. Adjust your walking gait a bit – no marching." It was an amusing first start to their meeting.

The group then huddled over the district map of Sandakan that was spread on the table.

"This Division is vast. Not all access roads are shown here, and we may have to use unpaved roads or *jalan tikus* (illegal pathways), as the locals call them, to get to our destinations. We may also have to face river crossings. GPS will be our mainstay when we move about. At some point in time, we need to traverse the famous Kinabatangan River to get to the villages. Something tells me that this might be sooner than we think," said Zain.

"A cruise on the river is then very much on the cards?" asked Su Eng. The question was rhetorical, but the idea was greeted with a loud cheer and clapping from the others.

Zain next turned his attention to the Tawau map in his possession.

"This map is not a detailed one, but it appears that this Division is also inundated with rivers and dense forests. We may be forced to recruit some locals as watchdogs. There are a lot of illegal migrants and Hakka speaking Chinese here I'm told. How are you with Hakka, pahlawan Su Eng?"

"I can understand the dialect, but am not fluent," replied Su Eng, smiling away.

"The same here," responded Zain, to everyone's surprise. "In any case, our intelligence gathering cannot be just confined to urban areas, but must also include several coastal villages and those in the interior regions of both Sandakan and Tawau."

A pause, before Zain continued. "But before we make any moves, I have arranged for us to have a security briefing at the Sandakan Police HQ this afternoon to get some first-hand information on ground realities. It is possible that the OCPD, Assistant Commissioner Arshad, may have invited the director of SCSC's Armed Forces Operational Centre, Brigadier General Othman Basiron to be present as well at our meeting. They have both been apprised by MinDef about our covert mission here to identify and disseminate all terror cells we might find, and in the process prise out the ISIS strongman Saadam from his hideout. If anyone else enquires about your status, simply state that you are a member of a team from MinDef on a logistics appraisal trip."

"Do you suspect our adversaries might be aware of our presence here?" asked Samy.

"They may have had some hint of my recruitment in this mission from their spies at MinDef, but it's unlikely that they could have gotten to know you all just yet. In any case, we should be on our guard and never underestimate the enemy. Make sure you don't leave any evidence that might relate to our mission in the open and unsecured in your rooms every time you step out. You can rest assured it will be a matter of time before others start trailing us.

"Let us now synchronise our watches and ensure that all the key and sensitive information that was given to us remains locked in as encrypted data in our smartphones. Remember that utmost secrecy must surround our mission. Our survival depends on it. That should not, however, deter you from interacting with the locals on your own. I hope I'm clear on this."

The pahlawans nodded. That done, the meeting soon disbursed, with the group agreeing to meet later at Police HQ.

CHAPTER 4

*T*he Sandakan Police HQ was an imposing white and blue-coloured building. As pre-arranged with the pahlawans, Zain entered the building first. Several police officers clad in dark clothes and bulletproof vests were just then bringing in a group of people in handcuffs. Some civilians in the vicinity who were taking a video on their phones of the unfolding scene were quickly pushed aside and warned their phones would be confiscated if they did not switch them off.

Zain moved away towards a quiet corner where he sought and received directions to the office of Assistant Commissioner Mohd.Arshad. He promptly signalled the pahlawans to enter the building. They climbed the stairs to the third floor where they were ushered into a waiting room. They did not have long to wait.

Arshad strode into the room apologising for the slight delay and invited them all to a large briefing room a few doors away from where the conference table was already laid out with coffee, tea, and several types of local kueh (cakes).

"A warm welcome to all of you. Please help yourselves to the refreshments. Our briefing will be in two stages. First, let me introduce you to Brigadier General

Othman Basiron. He is the director of SCSC's Armed Forces Operational Centre, and will give you the big picture of the external security threat issues in Sandakan and Tawau. Then I shall brief you on the specific security problems we are encountering in and around the Sandakan town."

Zain followed suit, introducing the pahlawans and stating that they will be primarily concerned with identifying sleeper cells, unearthing clandestine activities, and nefarious plans of insurgents in the state. "We are also permitted to undertake commando raids, but these will be with the full knowledge of SCSC. Keeping our anonymity intact, therefore, is critical for the success of our mission here. I'm sure you will understand." Both Othman and Arshad nodded their assent.

Brigadier General Othman then began his briefing by noting that an air of complacency about security had set in because of a sharp drop in kidnapping cases in recent months.

"It's only a lull resulting from our imposition of the dusk-to-dawn sea curfew. The moment we lift it, and what with the world economy spiralling down, it's only a question of time before the kidnappers resume their activities from the Sulu archipelago in the Philippines. Their modus operandi involves using speedboats under cover of night to target victims at coastal centres where there are eateries or on the tourist islands off Sandakan, like Selingan (Turtle Island) or Lankayan.

"The kidnappers rarely go into inland areas, but we find a new breed of water-borne criminals has now entered the scene. These are the provocateurs like we had during the 1963–1966 Indonesian Confrontation, and other radical elements. Indications are that they are venturing deep into the interior villages by the river route and instigating the people there to break away from Malaysia to reinstate the Sulu State. The worry is compounded by the fact that Islamic fundamentalists are also active in their midst."

Listening to this, Zain was reminded of his recent brush with conspirators and lurking sympathisers of the banned Al-Ma'unah group in peninsular Malaysia.

"We were informed that a special operations force of the Royal Navy, SINGA, has been charged with the task of monitoring the seas of Eastern Sabah. That's a vast stretch. Is there a naval base in Sandakan where they operate from?" asked Zain.

"Yes, they have a base here. I can arrange a visit for you later this evening if you wish to go there," responded Brigadier General Othman.

"We'll welcome that very much, sir," responded Zain, with some glee in his voice.

Arshad had more criminal activities and acts of sabotage on his plate of worries. "Smuggling is a big ongoing business in Sandakan, from drugs to turtle eggs to trapped wildlife. The police are kept on their toes all the year round. Another vice is money laundering. This has recently turned into a brisk activity here that we need to stamp out. A shadow Labuan offshore centre has been created here with a growing list of local contacts surreptitiously serving the interests of Sabah-based timber tycoons and a multitude of Indonesian and Bangladeshi foreign workers in peninsular Malaysia. How much of this money laundering has its connections with pro-IS extremists is an angle that remains to be investigated."

"I'm sure MinDef would appreciate some preliminary leads from you of organisations that are already on your radar," said Zain, giving Arshad an exaggerated wink.

At the end of the meeting, Zain sought a private moment with both Arshad and Othman to enlist their urgent help in finding a suitable bungalow house in a quiet setting in Sandakan to meet the accommodation needs of his teams and to serve also as their safe house while in Sabah. Othman promised to look into this and get back to Zain within a couple of days.

Leaving the building, Zain and the pahlawans took a stroll along the coastal road towards Harbour Square. They had slightly more than an hour to kill before their rendezvous with Brigadier General Othman at the Harbour Mall for the visit to the naval base. They had not walked far when an excited Dhanyal drew their attention to a large commercial poster advertising the Ocean King Seafood Restaurant. The restaurant was the scene of the widely reported kidnapping of a Sarawakian engineer by members of the Abu Sayaff violent jihadist group – and his subsequent beheading in the Philippines for failing to meet the ransom demands. The pahlawans resolved unanimously that they would have their dinner that night at the restaurant after their naval base visit.

The visit to the naval base at Sandakan took barely two hours. Zain and his team received a thorough briefing from Rear Admiral Datuk Selvarajah on the base's critical role in preserving the security of the maritime waters, particularly along Sabah's east coast, and of its enhanced functions since the shift of the Naval Region 2 HQ operations to Sandakan from Kota Kinabalu. The rear admiral and his two compatriots talked excitedly of their pending plans to shift to a more expansive location, as the current base was too close to the township.

Zain enquired of them about the facilities at the base and was told that they had several patrol boats and combat boats, as well as a few silver-breeze boats to undertake swift, short-term tasks. He was also told that the base would soon be receiving a couple of dozen or more high-tech, bulletproof, rigid-hull fender boats to be shared with the police, armed forces, and the Malaysian Maritime Enforcement Agency for undertaking maritime security missions.

Zain came away from the meeting convinced of the professionalism and commitment of those staffing the base to provide requisite protection to fishermen and others on the coastline of the districts of Beluran, Kinabatangan, and Sandakan, and parts of the Kudat and Tawau Divisions. But he felt that for surveillance that stretches to the farthest limits of territorial waters and offensive strikes against intruders, radar and satellite-beckoned air cover support had to be an integral part of such operations.

CHAPTER 5

*T*he next day, Zain gathered his two teams again in the guesthouse function room to work on their modus operandi.

"We shall work on the assumption that our enemy No.1 Saadam is already here in Sabah. To fulfil his evil agenda, he would very much need the support of Bangsamoro insurgents who have already made inroads here and cultivated local links. Being new to the land, he will, at least initially, feel more secure in their midst. Our game plan has to be based on this premise. We, therefore, have to cover the stretch between Sandakan and Tawau in search of clandestine terror cells....."

"That's quite a stretch! How do we do that?" interrupted Azlan.

"Through surreptitiously gathering intelligence data on fresh migrant arrivals, illegal movements of firearms, phone tapping, GPS tracking of suspects, and the like," explained Zain.

"I agree, we have to employ all possible ways," said Samy, with others nodding their assent as well.

"We need to settle on a strategy for hunting our man. Perhaps we should begin by classifying the main threats and the quarters they come from, the surveillance mode we need to adopt, and see where that leads us first," opined Zain.

Zain then reached for the whiteboard. He drew five columns and titled them:

THREAT | SOURCE[1]: | TARGET[2]: | SURVEILLANCE[3]: | REMARKS

[1]*Land/Sea;* [2]*Locations;* [3]*Mode*

"Let's work on this template, shall we? I have added the extra column named remarks so we can add special points here, such as objectives, asset recruiting, secret rendezvous points, preferred actions, like coordination with police/armed forces, infiltration into enemy ranks, hostage seizing, surgical strikes, etc. Any questions before we start on this? And, oh, by the way, I have arranged with MinDef to provide us with two cars for our transport needs with paid-for coupon cards for refuelling. They will all be 4-wheel drives. We should get them by this evening." The news was received with a loud cheer from all present.

The group then immersed themselves in the exercise for virtually the whole day. They explored several operational options, the safeguards that needed to be taken, and inter-group communication modes for real-time tracking of surgical strikes that may be executed. They also engaged in a mind game on the tactics that militants might deploy for side-stepping CASH's security net.

"If we were them, this is what we might want to do. We would sneak in by sea at nightfall in the monsoon months at different points on the coast and make our way to pre-identified areas inland that are somewhat isolated. Here we would quickly establish small village dwellings of our own, and engage in some asset recruitment among the Suluks, Bajaus, and southern Filipino Muslims. These dwellings will then be our entrenched bases, or cells, from where we shall launch our operations in surprise simultaneous attacks on targets elsewhere to spread terror. Our targets will be security establishments, places of worship, and community centres. Our 'hit list' will also include kidnapping and killing of key police personnel and counter-terrorism officers. We can be at our destructive best operating this way. The security forces will find it difficult to enforce wide-scale dusk-to-dawn land curfews, as this will earn them the wrath of locals." The view was expressed by Kamal, earning him appreciative nods all around.

"That's simply awesome! Just make sure you don't switch camps. If you do, I'll come for you with a big needle!" said Su Eng, to laughter from the crowd.

The exercise was extremely useful for formulating their action plans for their mission in Sabah for the first three months. It was agreed that the plans would be subject to periodic reviews.

"We have two days of stay left in this guesthouse. I guess we shall engage in some scouting around Sandakan this afternoon, and in Beluran, which is some 80 kilometres away, tomorrow before we plan and embark upon our covert mission," said Zain.

At the end of the meeting, the pahlawans made a beeline to the coffee house where Zain received the news that he could collect the cars that had been ordered for his teams through SCSC. Just as he was breaking the news to his teams, there was a call from Brigadier General Othman informing him that a Sandakan abode had been arranged for them at the government staff quarters enclave in Labuk Road.

Leaving their half-finished glasses of coffee, Zain and the pahlawans rushed to the showroom of the Proton car distributor in town. An official from SCSC was already waiting for them at the office of the manager to oversee the receipt of their official cars – two Mitsubishi Outlanders – and to attend to relevant documentation. The cars came equipped with satellite radio, Bluetooth, a USB port, keyless entry, and touchscreen GPS navigation – accessories well-suited for their needs.

After taking the cars for a spin, they headed for the government staff quarters enclave to check out an unoccupied old colonial building that was once the home of the Public Works Department (PWD) resident engineer. The enclave was not far from the State Secretariat building on Labuk Road. They went past the security entrance and located the house without much difficulty.

"You will find the key in a plastic bag underneath the big bougainvillea flowerpot at the porch entrance," was the message that Zain had received from Othman.

Parking their cars on the building's spacious grounds, they located the key and entered the premises. They found the place surprisingly dust-free, with the tables, chairs, and beds covered by protective plastic sheets. There were an old fridge and a gas stove in the kitchen; also, some cutlery in one of the drawers. There were electricity and water supply. They let the taps run in the kitchen and the bathrooms for a while, as the initial outflow from the taps was very muddy.

The pahlawans liked the house, as it was in a guarded enclave, well away from other buildings. They checked to see whether the place was free of hidden cameras and listening devices before pitching to spruce up the place. It was clear to them that the place had not been inhabited for several years. One of them remarked that their safe house is referred to as *Rumah Hantu* (Ghosthouse). The suggestion was unanimously accepted.

"We shall have to make duplicate keys to this place, and also have new padlocks installed at the front and back entrances. We shall do this today after we grab our lunch in town," said Zain.

"Perhaps we should get some toiletries for this place, and also minimally stock up the kitchen and fridge with some non-perishable items," added Su Eng, to a chorus of approval from the others.

"Ha-ha. I get the message. We have to dash first to the bank! Let's move out then," responded Zain, making for the door, followed by the others.

The stroll through various parts of Sandakan town after lunch proved a useful experience. The majority of the town's population was comprised of non-Malaysian citizens hailing from the southern Philippines. They were, like the Malays, Bajaus, and Suluks, counted as Muslims. The Chinese segment of the population, which was the business community, were mostly Cantonese and Hakka who had settled there during the colonial period.

Tasked to engage verbally with the residents, they presented themselves as social scientists working for the Sabah Kinship Foundation wanting to get a sense of people's sentiments on the economy and current affairs, all on a random and impersonal basis, with no names, photographs, or recordings being taken for the purpose. They followed the general guidelines for the modus operandi that they had discussed earlier for such verbal interactions, with only one member of each group being permitted to don the video-camera sunglasses that could be surreptitiously activated when needed. The selected "interviewees" would be ideally single persons, but no more than two, and those that may be found largely at food stalls and bus terminals.

The pattern of interviewing was simple. First, a disarming conversation was struck with each interviewee on the impact of the nation's declining economy on their livelihood in the state. Next, they were addressed with some straightforward questions to assess their level of contentment in infrastructure development in the state and on prevailing inter-ethnic relations within the community. The final segment of questions was to get their response to hypothetical questions bearing on Sabah's independent existence in the manner of Brunei, the reinstatement of a Sulu sultanate, and the possibility of the establishment in Sabah of an Islamic State.

An interviewee that raised strong suspicion to any group of being an informer or a potential saboteur in the making was to be presented with a ballpoint pen as a gift by the group's commander. Unknown to the recipients, each ballpoint pen carried a concealed micro GPS tracking chip.

There was no contact among the two groups for the entire day until evening when they all assembled in the Villa Permai guesthouse to exchange information and assess the effectiveness of their overall strategy in intelligence gathering. They decided to spend the night at the guesthouse and check out in the morning after breakfast.

Arriving at the Ghosthouse the morning after, they spent

some time cleaning up the place as insisted upon by the two ladies in their group.

"Where in Beluran are we heading?" asked Kamal.

"To some villages around Pekan Beluran," answered Zain.

"Through SCSC, I have contacted the Member of Parliament at Pekan and explained to him that we are a poll team working for the State Welfare Department gathering some inputs for villagers' welfare. He has kindly agreed to arrange for boat crossings where needed, and a guide to accompany us as well to a few villages populated largely by Kadazan – Dusun, Sungai, Tidung, Bajau-Suluk, and Rungus."

"That's quite an ethnic mix," noted Kamal.

"That's how it is in Sabah. Although some villages may have a dominance of one ethnic group over others, the harmonious mixing of groups here is something to marvel at, as you will all see," remarked Sungkiah. The conviction in her voice was not lost on others.

"I'll drink to that. Peninsula Malaysia, on the other hand, remains stuck in a racial quagmire," said Samy. "By the way, are these villages that we are visiting just fishing villages?" he inquired.

"Not entirely. The villagers engage in both fishing and agriculture. But many are handicapped by the absence of electricity and piped water supply. Also, they have limited or no access to basic resources such as roads, education, and health. This is especially so in Beluran and the Interior Division. Not the case for most villages in the more developed West Coast Division where I come from," noted Sungkiah.

"You're right. The villages are also home to many stateless citizens. Because of their discontentment with the state of affairs, it is conceivable that some of them may become easy targets for exploitation by dissident groups," observed Zain.

"Maybe so, but if you ask me, the vulnerability to ideological gibberish and mercenary recruitment by clandestine groups are not just with the poor only. Many of the educated youth in our country are also falling prey to extremist propaganda. And here I'm speaking from a religious perspective," said Kamal, who hailed from the state of Pahang in Peninsular Malaysia. 'Would you believe it, my own nephew dropped out of medical school in Egypt to join ISIS in Syria. The whole family is devastated.'

"I can empathise with that. To some extent, I blame the mainstream media for this. Their style of reporting has led to the rising spread of Islamophobia, which inadvertently is aiding the recruitment of young unwitting Muslims by the militants to fight for their cause. But getting back to our visits today, how do we contact our guide?" asked Samy,

"He will be waiting for us at the government rest house in town," replied Zain.

"We may gain some leverage over the villagers if we treat some of their sick people. Shall I pack some of our medicine along, just in case?" asked Su Eng.

"Good idea. You never know. It might help us later in asset recruitment," replied Zain.

It was a wet journey all the way. It was close to 1.00 p.m. when they finally arrived at the government rest house where they met their guide and availed of the set lunch that was served. The rain had begun to recede by then. With the help of their guide, they selected three villages for the visit. One of them, which was a bit more interior, entailed a river crossing.

The village heads were cooperative. They allowed the teams to randomly pick individuals whom they could converse with either in Malay or English. Almost all the villages had some sick people, including children. Su Eng had her hands full treating them and offering advice on sanitary hygiene. She immediately won the hearts of the villagers.

Going by the responses to the questions posed to them, it was clear that the sympathies of only one village were tilted towards the restoration of a Sulu sultanate.

One villager who was staying with his relatives in a Rungus longhouse (*vinataang*) confessed that they'd had "visitations" from the BIFF group some months back to garner support for the Islamic State. He slipped momentarily into one section of the longhouse to bring back a pamphlet they had distributed. He said he was not as enamoured by them as some of the younger villagers, as their idea of bringing back the Suluk sultanate of old was through instigating and executing widespread terrorism.

Zain immediately singled him out as a possible local recruit for his group, and discreetly arranged to get his particulars through a free medical check-up at the hands of Su Eng. He had to be sure this was not a case of planted counterintelligence on the part of the adversary. The young man's name was Jamil.

The rounds on the three villages were finally over by 7.00 p.m. The sun was already setting when they started their drive back to Sandakan. Some forty minutes into the journey, when they were nearing the Kabili-Sepilok Forest Reserve along Route 22, the car ahead driven by Kamal suddenly skidded with a burst tyre. Luckily, he managed to control it to a safe halt. But before he could get out, the unmistakable sound of gunshots ripped the air. Bullets smashed into his car, fired by an unseen enemy from the jungle fringe of the road. It was an ambush.

Kamal and his fellow pahlawans in the car, Dhanyal and Azlan, found themselves pinned down by the enemy, unable to get off the car. Samy, who was at the wheel of the second car some 100 metres behind, immediately hit the brakes and jumped out. Zain, Sungkiah and Su Eng quickly followed suit. Opening the car boot with the remote key, Samy retrieved their powerful M-16 assault rifles. They all fired non-stop at the muzzle flashes they could see in the tree line. The distraction allowed

Kamal and the fellow pahlawans to crawl out from the shielded side of their car and shoot back at the enemy using their pistols. The exchange of fire, however, didn't last long as the enemy left the scene as abruptly as they had appeared. Except for Kamal, who had a graze gunshot wound on his arm, none of the pahlawans suffered any injury. Su Eng treated his arm and kept him company in his car, with Azlan now at the wheel. Both the cars then drove away from the scene for some three kilometers before they stopped to replace the burst tyre of Kamal's car. The skirmish certainly had come out of the blue. But it was enough to warn the pahlawans that the enemy was aware of their mission and was already on their trail.

"Samy's quick reaction certainly saved the day for us," observed Su Eng, reflecting on the ambush. Both Azlan and Kamal nodded their agreement.

"He was awarded a police gallantry medal not so long ago. He is a guy who thinks on his feet, and earned a reputation for being a no-nonsense tough cop in his dealings with drug cartels," reminisced Kamal.

"He was also very much responsible for demolishing two feared gangs, one in Klang and the other in Kepong, who were blatantly extorting protection money from businesses there," chipped in Azlan. "Not a guy on whose wrong side you would ever want to be."

"Ha-ha, I hope the Sabah intruders get to know that too," said Su Eng, with a smile playing on her lips.

On their return to Ghosthouse, the pahlawans spent several hours checking the functionalities of their spyware and communication channels, and also going through their action plans. They decided that PP1 would head the next morning towards Lahad Datu, some 175 kilometres away to the south, while Group PP2 would operate in the Sandakan and Kudat Divisions.

"I shall go along with PP1," said Zain. Then turning to Kamal, he reminded him to get the bullet damaged doors of his car done up before leaving the perimeter of Sandakan.

Next, addressing the pahlawans generally, Zain said, "Catching illegal immigrants on land or at sea, an ongoing affair in the state, is not our concern, but that of SCSC. They are working on the matter in tandem with the police and immigration. Our top objective is to catch the kingpins who are propagating the Islamic State by helping insurgents establish terror cells with laundered money that gets them both recruits and firearms. You can be sure some deviant Islamic groups are at the back of this. They often propagate their ideology through their chosen Imams and provocateurs masquerading as members of many civil protest groups. And the police know that. In circumstances where the police cannot be seen to act pre-emptively, we can play that role." There was an air of finality in Zain's words that was not lost on the pahlawans.

"How exactly do we catch them?" The question came from Su Eng.

"We have to explore all options. We need to fish out information first, as we intend to do, by talking to villagers and town dwellers who had experienced insurgency incursions. Then we act on the information. This could mean following the trail of known racketeers and suspects indulging in gun-running and money laundering, tracking one or two of their members, and even kidnapping one or more of them."

"Kidnapping?" asked Su Eng, unbelievingly.

"Yes, but you resort to it only if you cannot access the information you want remotely from their mobile phones. Remember, all your phones have been installed with the remote cell-spy-stealth software. This is an incredible piece of software that allows you to spy on all their calls, messages, emails, media files, photos, etc. You can even trace their locations, if their phones are GPS-enabled. For accessing their phones, you need to surreptitiously get hold of their phone number first. Kidnapping is to price out more detailed or specific information, such as the whereabouts of their terror cells; to engage in this, we need the cooperation of the police," replied Zain.

"Getting an adversary's phone number without his knowledge is a tough ask," observed Dhanyal.

"Yes, indeed. It all depends on the circumstance and the place, whether the adversary is with a boisterous crowd or seated quietly at a table with others. What needs to be done is to steal very stealthily your target's mobile phone for a moment, or arrange for someone else to do that for you, and quickly move away from the scene. You will find that the phone is not often in a locked state so that you can get hold of the number readily from the "settings" icon. Otherwise, you'll have to wait till the phone rings, be deliberately incoherent and ask, 'what's the number you are trying to call, sir?' Hopefully, one person in ten will repeat the number. Then go back and leave the phone at the nearest place where it can be found by the original owner," replied Zain.

"Looks like you have practised this phoney art well. Pun intended!" quipped Su Eng.

At that point, Sungkiah drew their attention to the breaking news she was receiving on her mobile phone from her colleague serving at the military camp at Lok Kawi. The message read, "Petrol bomb hurled at a church in Ranau. Many killed. Police suspect criminals to be members of BIFF".

"The place is not far from Tuaran where I come from. Wish I could get these insurgents in my line of fire," she added ruefully.

"Well, pahlawans, our mission here is certainly not going to be a walk in the park. We all know about the collective glee of these religious miscreants when they strike down all those seen by them as *kafirs*. Let us be diligent and careful in our tasks. You don't have to rush into any acts of bravado. May the Almighty bless our mission and preserve us whole," said Zain.

"*Alhamdulillah* (Praise be to God)," was the phrase on everyone's lips before they retired for the night.

CHAPTER 6

*I*t took approximately three hours for Zain and his team to reach Lahad Datu. They headed straight for the Merdeka Bliss Hotel where Zain had booked two rooms.

After an early lunch, they made two quick visits to SCSC's military base and the police headquarters. The visits were pre-arranged with Brigadier General Othman while they were in Sandakan. Zain secured from the military base a detailed map of the Tawau Division indicating principal coastal and inland villages with road connections. Along with that, he gathered some information on the villages that had suffered previous insurgent incursions. He had an inkling that some of these villages might soon come under his scrutiny.

Visiting the police headquarters, he had the opportunity to touch base with his Tawau contact, Assistant Commissioner of Police (ACP) Rosmah Binti Yahaya. Being told that she was SCSC's director of intelligence, Zain decided to take her into his confidence, and explained the reason why he and his two teams were operating as undercover agents in Sabah. From her, Zain sought some sensitive information about major criminal gangs operating in Lahad Datu and elsewhere. In particular, he wanted access to confidential police records of ring leaders in gunrunning, drug trafficking, and money laundering. He was told that they could not be caught in the police net because of the lack of hard evidence against them, and this had emboldened them to expand their business links beyond the state. Zain was promised the information within a day or two by ACP Rosmah.

When they got back to their hotel, they were surprised to see a boisterous group had already assembled in the foyer, with many holding placards written in Arabic. They had all come to hear a public debate by a panel of four speakers, organised by a local university, in the hotel's large conference room. The title (translated from Malay) read: "*Resolving the impasse in the two-state solution to the Israeli-Palestinian conflict: Should Jerusalem become a city-state?*"

The start of the debate was set for 7.00 p.m., which was slightly more than an hour away. Zain noticed the conference room was yet unopened. He appreciated that this was for security reasons.

Looking at the motley crowd, Zain could sense anti-Zionist fervour building up among several groups. Would there be militant elements among them, was a question that immediately entered his mind.

Quickly calling his team aside to the lift entrance area, he whispered to them, "This debate here may be a God-sent opportunity for us. I want you, Dhanyal and Azlan, to go up quickly to your rooms, put on some minimal facial disguise, and then come down wearing your skull caps. We shall wait for you here."

Within moments, Zain's order was fulfilled, and the men in disguise came down. Zain continued with his instructions. "I want you both to disperse into sections of the crowd and listen intently to what is being said. Single out those who are speaking with a Tagalog accent, and those who are airing overtly religious statements. While you Azlan engage your target in friendly conversation, Dhanyal will descend on the scene whom you will pretend to hail as an old acquaintance. You will then request Dhanyal to take a picture of you with the target, and when handing over your cell phone note with some disgust that your phone has run out of charge. On the spur of the moment, Dhanyal, who will have his phone in silent mode hidden in his pocket, will request for the target's phone to take a few snapshots. But before handing it back, Dhanyal will give a missed call to his phone, and then quickly erase the call. Is that clear? Good, let's move in."

The debate started on the hour. It was a lively debate, with the speakers supporting the motion, however, having to contend with continued jeers from the biased audience. The order had to be restored several times during the proceedings by the chairman, who appealed to them to be open-minded. The din only quietened when police personnel who were on standby outside the hall entered and took up positions along the inner walls of the hall.

Just before the start of the debate, Zain had stationed all his three pahlawans outside the hall, as a group had suddenly sprung up there armed with banners and collection bins to raise funds in support of Palestinian refugees. He recalled warning his team about how such groups could be infiltrated by militants or their informants. He hoped that the pahlawans would be able to sense from their conversational engagement some bad elements among the crowd, although it was a tall order.

Following the end of the debate around 9.00 p.m., Zain met the pahlawans in his room to assess the fruits of their labour. He was pleasantly surprised to learn that they'd managed surreptitiously to pull five phone numbers 'out of the hat' just by mingling with the crowd.

Together, they spent the better part of an hour going through each of the numbers and finally noted with some glee that two of the numbers, including one that came from the group staging the Palestine refugee fundraising campaign, shed information pointing to criminal intent and sabotage. It was clear to them that to glean more revealing information, they needed next to tap the list of contacts that the two hacked phone numbers revealed, scan through old messages, and also eavesdrop on conversations in real-time.

They agreed to spend much of the following day looking into this.

It was an elated Zain that came out of Police HQ the next evening after he met with ACP Rosmah. The name list she gave of criminal offenders who had escaped arrest was going to be useful. He intended to match their names with the trail of contacts stealthily discerned from the hacked phone numbers the previous day.

Back in the confines of his room, Zain and his team tried to piece together the information they'd gleaned from the messages and eavesdropped bits of conversation, much of it in Malay, sourced from the interlinkages of the hacked phones. The following words "smuggling, drugs, firearms and ransom" cropped up on several messages, but what was intriguing were two places repeatedly mentioned in the conversation between one individual and two others. These were the names of the islands of Pulau Jambongan and Pulau Sebatik.

"Don't these two islands fall under CASH?" asked Dhanyal

"They sure do. If they are to be stealth landing destinations for the infiltrators, they have strategized well," responded Zain.

"How so?" asked Dhanyal.

"Jambongan is one of the largest islands in Malaysia. Perhaps SCSC assets there are inadequate to effectively comb the island's interior and coastal regions, and the enemy would have sensed that. A smaller island, on the other hand, would not provide much of an opportunity to the enemy for stealth landings," responded Zain.

"Don't forget also that Jambongan Island is located in Paitan Bay which has a few rivers flowing into it from the interior of Beluran. The rivers could be used by the intruders to make a fast getaway from the island," noted Sungkiah, who had a map in her hand.

"That's true. In the case of Pulau Sebatik, this is a divided island between Malaysia and Indonesia. Landing on the Indonesian side would allow them to cross over to Sabah, as the border is not patrolled at all," replied Zain, somewhat pedagogically.

Zain then contacted Kamal from the room and apprised him of the events of the past two days. He told him to take to take his team first to Paitan town in Beluran district, and from there to make their way by boat to Pulau Jambongan.

"The villages on this island are inhabited by the Bugis and Suluk people. Find an excuse for your visit and try to sniff out if there is anything odd about to happen there. I suspect infiltrators are planning to set up a landing base somewhere on the island with the help of one group of villagers. There is a township on the southeast corner of the island with the same name. I'm not sure if you can find accommodation there; otherwise, you may have to operate from Paitan."

"In fact, we were planning to go to Kudat by road via Paitan and Maruda Bay. No problem breaking journey in Paitan," responded Kamal.

"That's good! By the way, there's another island here, down south, which we intend to survey. It is Pulau Sebatik. The island is divided between Malaysia and Indonesia. We suspect some cross-border gunrunning activity could be rife on this island. We plan to go there soon."

Turning next to the pahlawans in the room, Zain said, "Our first port of call tomorrow is at Kampung Kerinchi. The police had once raided this village in search of drug traffickers. We cannot be certain they all have disappeared from the village. From there, we shall go to Kampung Hell."

"What!" exclaimed Azlan.

"That's the other name for Kampung Attap, once the disadvantaged area of Tawau noted for gangsterism."

CHAPTER 7

*T*he night was unusually dark. Moisture-laden clouds hung low in the sky, blocking visibility of any stars. The dim streetlights cast sombre shadows that quivered in the wind that came from nowhere. The heavy swaying of palm trees and the rattle of empty bottles and tins littered at the roadsides signalled an ominous weather change. The howling of dogs added to the din, scurrying home the few pedestrians on the roads who had but only a month ago witnessed the gruesome impact of Tropical Storm Vinta.

The guards manning the gates that night at the Zamboanga city port flagged down the two trucks that were approaching the area. The trucks bore the stamp of Filipino military, although the driver and his assistant in each truck wore civilian clothes and sported only army caps. The guards inspected the documents carried by the two drivers along with the padded sealed envelopes slipped into their hands. Following a cursory glance at the contents of the trucks from the back of the vehicles, they waved the trucks on.

"Berth 1 is where your cargo ship *Spirit of Celebes* is docked, bound for Sandakan," said one of the guards, pointing to the direction.

Arriving at the scene, the trucks unloaded several crates labelled 'Machinery & Transport Equipment.' They stood out against the multitude of other crates carrying fresh bananas, the country's second top export commodity, also bound for Sandakan.

Customs officers and a ship's official soon descended on the scene and were told of the contents of the crates detailed in the forged ISF (Importer Security Filing) document and the freshly prepared Bill of Lading that bore the name of Federal Cargo Express & Logistics Services as sender and Chong Yuen Engineering Works, Sandakan, as the buyer. Again, puffy, sealed window envelopes exchanged hands

The trucks left soon thereafter to a workshop in downtown Zamboanga, where the military coat of paint on them was meticulously removed.

"Everything went well?" asked a plump man sporting a Hard Rock Café Manila shirt.

"*Opo ginoo* (Yes, sir)," replied the men, who were hired for the job. They were frisked for hidden money on them, and the tracking gadgets hidden unknown to them on their shirts were removed. They were then paid off.

The plump man then went through with his associate the list of various items intended for clandestine gun manufacturing, all cleverly hidden with the rest of the machinery in the crates. These included, besides some essential gunsmith tools, a small CNC machine ("ghost gunner") designed to manufacture 80 percent lowers for

AR-15 (ArmaLite Rifle-15), and several basic upper and lower receiver parts kits. The plump man then made a quick call. His words were crisp. "Mario, the parcels have been sent. Your contact, CY, will be advised on the matter. Await instructions when you get there. Move with extreme caution."

Zain would have flipped if he had overheard the conversation, for the call was to the same Mario who had escaped capture when the clandestine gun factory he was establishing in Perak's Royal Belum Rainforest was raided. The hideout of the gun factory was uncovered by Zain.

Mario, who was in suburban Manila, suppressed his excitement at receiving the call. He had an unfinished agenda in Malaysia. He decided that his entry into Sandakan had to be by boarding the overnight ferry at Zamboanga along with a large group of other Filipino tourists. And he was on it eight days later.

As he walked towards the Malaysian immigration barrier, his nerves ragged with internal stress, he saw signs of danger everywhere. The immigration officer attending to him seemed to study his papers for an inordinate length of time, and wanted him to remove his cap and spectacles to face the camera one more time. He couldn't help breathe a sigh of relief when he was finally let through. He had carried with him a false letter of invitation to gain entry. The plastic surgeon in Manila had done a marvellous skin grafting job on his thumbs. He kissed his right thumb and quickly pulled it away from his lips at the exit. Not wanting to take any chances of being recognised, he pulled down his cap to cover his face as he made his way to the taxi stand.

"New Town Hotel at Leila Road, please," he said to the taxi driver.

Awaiting him at the hotel registration desk was Chong Yuen.

"Nice to see you. Was the trip OK?" he asked.

"A bit tiring. Left yesterday at one p.m. It took some 16 hours to cross the sea," replied Mario.

"Never mind. Take rest now. I have booked you a room here for 3 to 4 days. Think the shipment will arrive soon?" asked Chong, while handing Mario a file.

"Have you settled on the site for the assembly?" countered Mario.

"No problem. I have added a two-storey annex to my factory. You can safely operate from one of the floors. Shall come back later. Have to rush to my bank now. Got an important meeting," replied Chong, who then left the hotel.

Arriving at Kampung Kerinchi with his PP1 team, Zain decided to wield his newly acquired marvel – a *smelloscope* – while entering some village homes. He had arranged for its purchase through MinDef at the tail end of his last mission, having read about its success in the USA as a dual-purpose pot and breath analyser. He hoped the device would literally smell out *ganja* (cannabis) and syabu (methamphetamine) smokers hiding in the village. The villagers, unaware of its potency, would simply view it as a video recorder!

This time, their entry into the village was as masquerading health officers checking for Dengue mosquito breeding sites both within homes and in their immediate environment. This was a clever ploy on their part to ward off any suspicion.

Luck was riding with Zain when the smelloscope he was handling did more than its task; in two houses, they found drug addicts hiding away from the eyes of the law. There were two guys sprawled on the floor in the one house, virtually dead to the world, still in a whirl of their hallucinated dreams. In the second house, the drug victim was a teenager, half-naked, who was squatting on the floor. He had a sunken, emaciated face, and was not at all shamefaced when his parents spat vitriol at him.

Zain knelt near the boy, and zipping open the pouch attached to his trouser belt, he confiscated two small packets of syabu (methamphetamine). He then turned to his parents and consoled them of the very real possibility of curing him of his addiction. Working into their confidence, he elicited the name of the drug hustler. They warned him that the hustler could be armed and was probably part of a large Filipino-Chinese cartel that was operating from outside of Tawau.

The pahlawans continued with their rounds, extracting samples of stagnant water with turkey basters and collecting them in plastic bags, all in a show of pretence for mosquito larval analysis.

Later, speaking to the *ketua kampung* (village head), a sturdy, middle-aged man, Zain impressed upon him the need to rehabilitate the three drug addicts. In promising to keep the matter under wraps from the police, he extracted from him the name of the drug cartel. Voluntarily, the ketua kampung also showed them photographs from his cell phone of two foreigners who made periodic visits to the village, and mentioned the police had not taken any notice of his suspicion that they could be cartel frontmen. It was quite evident to Zain that this man was hinting that the police were being bribed.

The group then engaged him in a long and searching interrogation. His name was Nasri Abdurajak. They learnt from him that his father was the ketua kampung before him. When asked about his background, he mentioned having worked outside his village in cocoa and oil palm plantations, and of his travels to many parts of Tawau.

"Really?" asked Zain.

"Yeah! In fact, I was not far from the Tanduo village in Lahad Datu when Filipino Forces of the Sulu Sultanate attacked it in 2013."

"I remember reading about it..." began Zain, but an excited Nasri cut him short.

"The attack was sudden. They came by speedboats from an island in Tawi-Tawi, and caught everyone there by surprise."

"Do you feel that the Suluks and other Sabahans would welcome back a Sulu sultanate in Sabah?" asked Sungkiah, somewhat casually.

"No way. I'm part Suluk and part Bugis, but the Suluks here in Tawau have assimilated well with local Malays and Indonesians, and we don't want Filipino immigrants here which a Sulu sultanate will definitely attract. I'm sure the indigenous Kadazan-Dusuns and Muruts also would not favour this. I have some friends among them, and they fear that if a Sultanate emerges again, militants will soon convert it into an Islamic State," replied Nasri unflinchingly.

This was an answer none of them expected to hear from the village head.

"*Air yang tenang jangan disangka tiada buaya,* (Still waters run deep)," whispered Sungkiah to Zain, more in an appreciative vein.

"What about the Sama-Bajau? I understand they are the second-largest ethnic group in Sabah," provoked Sungkiah.

"Yes, you're right. They are not only large, but also a very diverse group. They speak many dialects, but have no common language to bind them into a political force. The majority of them are seafaring people, not land dwellers. In Tawau you find them mostly around Semporna. I don't think they would support a Sulu sultanate," replied Nasri.

"That's an interesting analysis. By the way, have you heard lately of the presence in Sabah of an ISIS leader provoking the establishment of an Islamic state?" asked Zain.

Nasri gave a blank look, prompting Zain to suddenly change the subject, and ask, "What are your plans for this village, as its ketua?"

"I have applied to get some government grant and assistance to start a village-level aquaculture business. I'm sure this will benefit us the most," replied Nasri.

"How did you come to know about this business?" enquired Zain.

"I read about it in the papers – a report on a solar PV and aquaponic farm that had been started at Kampung Sungai Kalumpang, near the Sipadan Mangrove Resort. I was thinking of a small-scale project along those lines here," replied Nasri.

Zain pondered over Nasri's response for a while. He appreciated his initiative and his level of general knowledge about current affairs in the state.

Getting meaningful nods from his mates, he turned to Nasri. "You have impressed us, Nasri. We are going to take you into our confidence. We are undercover agents working for the national counterterrorism centre, and our task is to sniff out big-time criminals and anti-national elements who are bent on bringing down our democratically elected government. If you are agreeable, we want to enlist your help in this and report to us any strong leads that we can follow up. You will have to be very vigilant, of course, not to arouse any suspicion on yourself, for the people you may run into are hardened criminals and killers; some may even be misguided jihadists. Naturally, you will be rewarded for any tip-offs that lead to the capture and arrest of one or more such people. Are you willing to be our shadow recruit?"

Nasri stroked his chin while looking intently at the group. Breaking into a smile, he then said, "You know, I have always wanted to be a cop.I can't believe you are giving me this chance, and a role to play to protect our state."

"Welcome aboard, then," replied Zain, gripping Nasri's hand in a warm handshake. Then, penning a number on his hand, Zain showed it to Nasri, saying, "Here, memorize this number, and if you have any information to give us, call this number thrice. It's a redirected call number. You will hear an alarm tone to indicate it has been received. It's also one-way communication. Your password when communicating the message will be *nyamuk* (mosquito). If we need to communicate with you urgently, we will resort to sending you a self-destructing audio message on your phone. We will now download this free app on your phone and show you how it works.That will be the arrangement for the present, at least. Is that clear?"

Zain then went about installing the Wickr app on Nasri's phone. Halfway through this, he nonchalantly asked Nasri for his Apple ID and password, which he quickly noted in his phone. That done, he returned Nasri's phone to him and asked him to call the number that he had been asked to commit to memory and send an encrypted message. Satisfied that Nasri had understood the instructions, the group then took their leave, after securing from him a few personal details.

"I hope we have not been hasty in recruiting him," said Azlan as they made their way to the next destination.

"Not to worry. We have his phone details to spy on his device and also track his movements," replied Zain.

Their next destination was several hours away at Kampung Attap, a village populated mostly by Indonesian and Filipino immigrants who had long domiciled there, most without proper documentation. They also learnt that the village had been administratively broken up into three sections – Kampung Attap Utara, Kampung Attap Tengah, and Kampung Attap Selatan. They decided to visit Kampung Attap Selatan, the remote section of the village. This appeared also to be the poorest section of the village, with many residing in illegal houses raised by stilts in the river. There was evidence of many such recently demolished houses ordered by housing inspectors from the Housing and Local Government Ministry, but it appeared that the villagers had no qualms in erecting them again.

The group interacted with the residents as tourists inquisitive about the pattern of their daily lives. They noticed that electricity supply was not available to most houses of the village, but there were streetlamps. A fair number of vehicles, they observed, were approaching and leaving the village. They gathered that many were there from Kampung Attap Tengah to set up the *pasar malam* (night market) on a nearly daily basis. They approached a fruit stall that was among the first to be set up. They found a heap of small fruits in a basket that looked like durians but smelled more like jackfruits. Sungkiah said they were called *tarap*, and that they were indigenous only to Borneo Island. She took a photograph of the fruit vendor splicing open the fruit for them to taste. Tasting the fruit, they all enjoyed its mild jackfruit creamy flavour.

Chatting next with a nearby sundry shop owner, they heard from him that his business was heavily undermined by the pasar malam. When asked for the reason, he said, "They bring in smuggled goods, including cigarettes and liquor, from Sungai Nyamuk in Indonesia and sell it cheaply here."

"How do they smuggle the items here?" asked Dhanyal.

"By speedboat late at night. It is only a short ride to get here from Sungai Nyamuk. The smuggled goods also get sold in Tawau town, which is about a few kilometres away," replied the shopkeeper.

Having also heard about the notoriety of Kampung Attap for gangsterism, the group was vigilant about shady characters making a beeline to them. But everything appeared to be normal on the streets, and they were making plans to return to Lahad Datu when five cars in a convoy suddenly entered the village and made their way to the river's edge. Witnessing the scene from a bend in the road,

Zain and his team saw a sack being pulled out from the trunk of a car. Two men hurriedly placed the sack in a boat and rowed it to a house on stilts. The cars and the men then left the village as hurriedly as they had come.

There were some bystanders at the water's edge witnessing the scene. Zain and his group approached them.

"What was all that about? Smuggled goods being hidden away?" asked Zain of the bystanders, but they simply shrugged their shoulders and walked away.

Entering the car, he retrieved some headgear and face masks, and asking Dhanyal to keep watch, beckoned Azlan and Sungkiah to join him. The three of them then stealthily entered a boat and rowed it to the house. With Azlan remaining guard on the boat, Sungkiah and Zain donned their headgear and face masks, and with pistols in hand, quietly entered the house. The room they first stepped into was in partial darkness, and no one seemed to be around. With their flashlight on, they moved deeper into the house and saw through a partially open door of a room a man seated on a chair, gagged, and with his hands tied together behind the chair. They realised at once that the bundle in the sack was this man, and it looked like a case of kidnapping for ransom.

There were two other persons in the room; one engrossed with his phone, and the other attempting to light a kerosene lamp. Too late, they realised the presence in the room of Zain and Sungkiah who quietened them to a corner at gunpoint. While Sungkiah stood to watch over them, Zain untied the hostage, an elderly Chinese male. Using the same rope, Zain then ordered the two men to be seated back-to-back and tied their hands together. Finding a large piece of cloth in the room, Sungkiah followed suit, tearing the cloth into long strands to gag them and tie their legs.

Turning to look at them before leaving the room, Zain said in a harsh tone in Malay, "*Jangan anda berani menculik orang kami!* (Don't you dare kidnap our man!)"

Descending into the waiting boat, Zain asked the hostage they had freed, "What's your name, and where are you from?"

"Teh Soon Hock. I'm from Tawau town. I run a timber firm," replied the man in a shivering voice.

"So they kidnapped you for ransom?"

"Yes, I heard them talking in the car about asking three million ringgits from my family for my release," replied Teh, who looked as if he was about to have a nervous breakdown.

"Don't worry. We're not a new batch of kidnappers, but undercover police," replied Zain, removing his face mask.

Back in their car with their released hostage, they sped quickly from the village towards Lahad Datu, which was some 150 kilometres away.

"We don't want to take you to Tawau, as your premises may still be under watch. I want them to think a rival gang has snatched you away from them," said Zain. He then immediately contacted ACP Rosmah and narrated to her the kidnapping they had foiled.

"I think he has to stay hidden for some time until you launch a raid on the illegal stilt house in the village, and get its occupants to reveal the names of the kidnappers. The kidnappers came to the village in five cars. I recall the number plate of one car. It's STA 3488A. I hope that gives you a lead."

"That's useful information. We should have no problems in tracing the car," responded Rosmah.

"What do we do with Teh? Shall we bring him over to you? And, oh, his family in Tawau town needs protection as well."

"We will arrange for his family's protection. But don't bring him here just yet. I cannot have him give any statement that exposes you and your team, you understand?"

"Perfectly. Thank you," responded Zain.

The long trip back allowed Zain to gain valuable information from a grateful Teh about dishonest loggers in Sabah who engage in overharvesting and illegal export.

"Are any politicians involved with these dishonest loggers?" It was a pointed question that Zain asked Teh.

"I know a couple of them are. I'm told they keep all their monetary transactions overseas to avoid local scrutiny."

"That is money laundering, if you ask me. But I'm sure that there has to be a trail locally that has not surfaced or received the scrutiny of the authorities," remarked Zain, who was in a probing mood.

Teh hesitated for a moment before responding in a soft voice, "I suspect the Sandakan branch of a foreign bank is the nexus for their money laundering."

Zain couldn't have wished for more first-hand information on the subject.

CHAPTER 8

*T*he next morning saw Zain seated in the lounge following an early breakfast with the *Daily Express* in his hands. He scanned the newspaper for reports of any internal and external threats that had been thwarted by SCSC. But there were none. Instead, the paper's headline screamed out a more imminent threat – SABAH PUT ON TSUNAMI WATCH. Zain read on to learn that there had been dozens of tremors over the past two weeks in Indonesia's Sulawesi and the Lesser Sunda Islands and the Philippines' Mindanao Island, with magnitudes ranging between 4.0 and 6.0 on the Richter scale. In the wake of this, the Malaysian Meteorological Department had issued a public alert of a possible tsunami arising in the Celebes and Sulu seas that could sweep Sabah's eastern coastline with little or no warning. Zain immediately placed a call to DCP Datuk Johari Sulaiman, the commander of SCSC.

"How serious is the tsunami threat? Will you have to curtail your maritime surveillance?" asked Zain as soon as Datuk Johari came on the line.

"I'm afraid we cannot ignore the tsunami warning and risk losing our vessels. We are in constant touch with the meteorological department," responded Datuk Johari.

Zain understood that to mean a severe curtailment of coastal vigilance. His detective mindset told him that extremist Moro infiltrators from the Philippines could well seize the moment to stage multiple coastal landings, as they had long toyed with the idea of establishing a land base in Sabah. It was a gamble that he would not hesitate to take if he were the enemy.

He rushed back to his room to examine the maps of the Sandakan and Tawau Divisions. He wanted to confirm the exact locations of the two islands whose names the pahlawans had overheard from the cell phones they had previously hacked – Pulau Jambongan and Pulau Sebatik. He double-checked their coordinates from the Google map using his cell phone. A web search revealed that the border of Pulau Sebatik was not patrolled, and there was also no immigration or customs checkpoints on the Malaysian part of the island on account of its proximity to Tawau. A clandestine base on the Indonesian part of the island, reasoned Zain, would provide militant groups ample opportunity to plan their stealth moves into areas in Tawau and beyond.

Could these two islands be the destinations for planned landings into Sabah? If so, from which islands in the Sulu archipelago in the southwestern Philippines would the marauders most likely embark? The principal islands in the archipelago, which stretches from the northern limit of the Celebes Sea to the southern limit of the Sulu Sea, include Jolo, Tawi-Tawi, Sanga-Sanga, Sibutu, Siasi, and

Cagayan Sulu. Common sense dictated that the chosen islands had to be at the edge of the international treaty limits separating the Philippines and Malaysia, but it was anybody's guess where the operational starts would commence from. If Pulau Jambongan was a target destination, Zain reasoned that Taganak Island, the largest in the Turtle Island group, was a likely embarking point, as indeed also any one of the islands in the Palawan archipelago in the southern Philippines. For entry into Pulau Sebatik, and perhaps also into Semporna, Zain picked Sibutu Island. He knew these were but only conjectures, and there was also no way of knowing whether infiltrations would occur or, indeed, might have already begun.

Zain rang up Datuk Johari again. "Based on our phone surveillance, we think that if the infiltrators are going to sneak in large numbers by sea into Sabah, their embarking points could conceivably include Taganak and Sibutu islands. Is there no way you can order your combat ships to sail close to the international maritime boundary and send drones to spy on any new harbour structures created on these islands? This would certainly give us a clue."

Datuk Johari was silent for a while before he came back on the line. "It's not impossible. We can arrange for a ship to give chase to a decoy speedboat fleeing to an island, and use that excuse to send a drone around the island."

"That's great, sir! I would like to discuss this further with you, if I may. Could we meet sometime tomorrow?"

"I may be tied up tomorrow; the day after would suit me fine, preferably in the afternoon. This is subject to there being no tsunami. I shall also get Brigadier General Othman to join us."

Zain gave no indication of Jambongan or Sebatik islands to Datuk Johari. He wanted to get some key information about these sites first from his teams. He then tried to contact Samy and Kamal, but the network connection eluded him.

Barely three hours after the issuance of the tsunami alert, another earthquake of 7.1 magnitudes hit central Sulawesi, preceded by a sequence of foreshocks, the largest of which was a tremor of the magnitude of 6.1 that was felt in parts of Tawau and East Kalimantan. The alert remained for another couple of hours before it was withdrawn.

At the news of the tsunami alert, Kamal and his PP2 team decided to delay their 220-kilometre trip to Paitan by a day. They also wanted to gather more information about their Jambongan Island destination from both the police and the tourist bureau. There was no indication whether there was a car ferry from Paitan to Jambongan Island, which meant there was a need to arrange for transport for moving about on the island. It was then that they learnt that a prominent West Malaysian plantations group had a palm oil mill operating on the island in their estate.

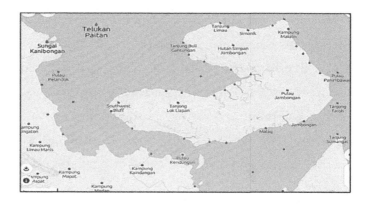

Map showing Jambongan Island and its location off Sabah's east coast

(Source: https://en.wikipedia.org/wiki/Jambongan_Island)

Samy suddenly remembered he had a friend who was the manager of the company's palm oil mill in Johor. Luck was on his side. His friend had just returned to his mill after a study visit to the Jambongan mill. His friend made arrangements for their two-day stay in the company's quarters, and also put a jeep at their disposal to move about.

The pahlawans set out the following day. It took them four hours to reach Paitan, driving on the pothole-ridden two-lane road. They booked into a hotel in town, and leaving their vehicle there, set out to Jambongan on a hired speedboat. It was a half-hour ride to the Pekan Beluran Jetty. They were greeted upon arrival by a man from the island's palm oil mill who drove them straight to the estate. A quick tour of the mill was organised for the

91

pahlawans before they were driven a short distance away to Jambongan town for dinner. They noted that the town had military and RELA posts, a rural clinic, and a police station.

Returning to the estate, they were ushered to the visitors' quarters. They were pleasantly surprised to find the place air-conditioned, with mosquito netting at all the windows. The kitchen had filtered drinking water, an electric kettle, and several "three-in-one" tea and coffee sachets.

Their contact man knocked on their door sharply at nine the next morning to announce that their jeep would be ready within the hour. Sipping their beverages at the kitchen table, the pahlawans decided they would spend the day examining the coastline stretches of the horseshoe-shaped island by jeep.

They first dropped by at the police station to secure information on the extent and reach of coastal roads on the island and the names of large villages on the path. They learned that there was only one trunk from the town and school jetty that winds its way westward to the one horseshoe edge at Southwest Bluff. Dirt roads linked to this trunk road provide access to fishing villages on the west coast, but east-coast villages, they were told, were bereft of any road link. It was further impressed upon them that the island was a part of CASH and incorporated six villages.

Reading the name list of the villages, Samy whispered to Kamal, "I cannot imagine the infiltrators would choose any of them to set foot on the island."

"You're right, but the list that they have given us also includes other villages we really ought to get to. I wonder whether they would be accessible by road. Perhaps we should charter a boat and go around the island," said Kamal.

"Yup, we ought to do that as well. The police did mention that Kampung Melalin and Kampung Lima-Limau can be accessed only by boat. We may be able to hire a motorboat at the school jetty or the nearby jetty at Kampung Hujung. But let's do the jeep ride first, and see whether we can get to meet at least some of the villagers on the west coast," responded Samy as they entered the jeep.

Their first port of call was at Kampung Sarip, which they reached by veering off the main road onto a dirt track. As they approached the village, they were spellbound by the scenic sight that met their eyes – the blue sea and the white, sandy shores struck them as too tranquil a setting to be turned into anything demonic, except by an unpredictable dastardly act of external aggression or a sudden lash-out by the fury of nature. There were stilt houses, some tattered on the waterline, and a jetty at which some boats were anchored.

Most of the boats were still out at sea, but the pahlawans got the opportunity to talk to a few village elders who were handling large lobsters from one of the fishing boats that had returned early with the morning's catch.

A Bajau stilt house on water *(Photo credit: John Jodeery via Flickr.com)*

They were piqued to learn from the villagers that all marine life caught for consumption should never, at least in the first instance, be roasted, but rather boiled. They subsequently learnt that it was a quaint custom or taboo observed by many villagers on the island. Engaging them deeper in conversation, the pahlawans gathered that they lived under the constant fear of being kidnapped and robbed at sea by foreign gunmen on trawlers and speedboats. They were aware that many villagers living on the mainland had suffered this fate. The consensus view among them was that security was not tight enough around the island and that a greater security presence was called for.

Re-joining the main road, they next moved to another village, Kampung Nibong, which was near the periphery of a mangrove forest. The houses there were also on stilts, raised from the ground to avoid flooding. These were in addition to a few stilt houses on water that were illegally erected at the coast. The villagers were mostly of the Tausug-Sulu ethnicity. While they all relied on rainwater for their water supply, for power, some of the houses had diesel-run generators which they switched on only at night to save costs.

The pahlawans were quick to note that the village mosque was having a facelift. Quizzed on this, the ketua kampung said they had some benefactors who had come to the village a few months back, and they now also had a new Imam. Intrigued, Kamal decided to pay a courtesy call on the Imam and pray at the mosque. It was a revealing discussion that he had with the Imam who was a young man of Suluk descent, with a degree in Islamic Studies. "My goal in life is to promote Islam and spread its true values among young Muslims by peaceful means. I abhor the spread of Islam by violence," said the Imam, looking at Kamal straight in the eye.

To Kamal, the Imam's words were just cliché. He asked him a few blunt questions. On the first question of whether he favoured a return of the Sulu sultanate in Sabah, the Imam was hedgy, saying political matters didn't concern him. On the second question of where the funds for the mosque renovation and his work in the village was coming from, he simply said it was the contribution of well-wishers, among them wealthy businessmen.

Kamal mulled over his replies and posed a third question, which was in a way a hybrid of the earlier questions: "How do you know that radical Islamic charities are not behind them, intent on creating an Islamic State here by overthrowing the government by political means, which is another form of jihad in their eyes?"

It was a loaded question. The Imam hesitated a while before answering, unsure now who his interrogator was. "We are careful with whom we interact. Our benefactors have no political links. The older generation of our clergy have not only become corrupt but have lost their clout. They are letting our religion be hijacked by vested interests." With those words, the Imam retracted to his room, as the alert on his phone reminded him of his prayer time. He asked Kamal to join him in prayers at the mosque later if he stayed on.

Coming out of the mosque, Kamal found Samy and Su Eng waiting for him. "Looks like there is some amount of internet coverage here. Perhaps we should see if the ketua kampung has a phone too, and hack it the usual way," said Su Eng. They were in luck. The ketua kampung indeed possessed a phone. At the pretext of taking a picture of him in front of the mosque using the man's phone, Su Eng surreptitiously used it to give a missed call to her phone, and once done, quickly erased evidence of that call.

"That was an interesting talk that I had with the Imam. I don't buy the story of wealthy businessmen coming here to do charitable work. It's a façade for something else; perhaps creating a haven here for some sinister activity," said Kamal as they left the village to resume their trip.

The stretches of the road on either side were flanked by oil palm plantations and secondary forests. They sighted some villagers on motorbikes appearing on the road from apparently nowhere and then disappearing into the thicket at places they assumed contained man-made tracks leading to fishing villages on the coast. They stopped an individual to enquire about the distance; he estimated the distance to be 3 to 4 kilometres. They parked the vehicle by the roadside and decided to follow him to the village, wearing their jungle trekking boots. These had drainage holes in the instep near the sole to allow water to flow out in the event they had to make a stream crossing.

The water village they entered was a small fishing hamlet with less than two hundred residents. The majority of them were Bugis people. They learnt that the villagers did much of their fishing in Paitan Bay, and only occasionally sailed out to the open Sulu Sea. The ketua kampung recounted to them a recent incident involving the abduction and subsequent release of some of the villagers while at sea by gunmen who had come in a large trawler boat. It seemed the gunmen were merely interested in usurping their fishing boats and the fish they had netted.

"Were the gunmen locals or foreigners?" asked Su Eng.

"They spoke Tagalog," replied the ketua kampung.

"Is it not possible they are planning to use the seized boats to enter the island without arousing too much suspicion?" asked Su Eng, turning to her mates.

"Most likely this is their intention as the local fishing boats are all required to have the automatic identification system installed in them. We need to take a motorboat ride around the island and look out for likely spots they may pick to land. I suspect that they may also seek shelter in small water villages near the horseshoe edges, as these would be nearer the mainland." The response came from Samy.

"I guess this will have to be tomorrow, then," said Kamal as he lined up with the others to watch in awe the rhythmic dance of the waves at the pristine beach.

Retracing their steps to their open jeep a while later, they found to their shock that some monkeys had already wandered into the vehicle and ransacked their plastic bags which contained some eatables. Su Eng, uttering some expletives in Chinese, gave them chase, much to the mirth of the others.

Back in their jeep, they drove on to the farthest point they could on the road and walked the remaining distance to Southwest Bluff. They had an exhilarating view of the bay, the island's hinterland, and of the mainland coast from their vantage position. They wouldn't have traded the moment for anything else in the world – that was their unequivocal opinion, before they turned their vehicle back for the return trip.

Overnight at their quarters, they managed to contact Zain and shared with him their observations.

"A boat surveillance of the island's coastline, indeed, seems warranted. Make sure, though, you jot down the coordinates of likely disembarkation points as you go around the island," was Zain's parting advice.

The next morning, the pahlawans left early and had little difficulty in getting the services of a boatman at the school jetty to take them around the island. They first entered Kampung Hujung, which was probably the best-endowed village on the island, with fewer stilt houses on the shoreline, and solar-powered electricity being available to most houses. Leaving the Bugis-dominated village after a short walk around, they headed for Kampung Melalin, another strong SCSC bastion. It was a village nestled on a hill overlooking the Sulu Sea, with a panoramic beach view. They encountered here one of the longest village jetties they had ever seen. The village was backward in facilities, but they were told by the villagers they met that a rural clinic had just been established there.

Su Eng expressed a desire to visit the clinic. Samy offered to accompany her, while Kamal decided he will take a stroll through the village and meet up with the ketua kampong. A narrow lane separated the two rows of thatched houses that faced each other. The row nearest the beach had a few longhouses facing the sea, perhaps being the earliest built. This was not the case with the others.

"You go in, I'll stay back here," said Samy as he and Su Eng reached the clinic's entrance. She met the hospital assistant who was in charge there. A fisherman who had sustained a deep cut on his leg and another suffering from excessive fatigue were the patients in the clinic at that moment, and Su Eng was more than happy to lend her assistance.

"Where are you from, doctor?" asked the medical assistant.

"I'm from Penang in Peninsular Malaysia," replied Su Eng. She didn't want the hospital assistant to be too inquisitive.

"I saw you hand your pistol to your friend before you entered the clinic," said the man.

A shocked Su Eng muttered 'Damn' under her breath. She recalled taking the gun temporarily off her concealed ankle holster while on the boat, and keeping it hidden in her medical bag, but had forgotten about it until she neared the clinic. She recovered quickly, however, to explain nonchalantly that she was an army doctor, licensed to carry her gun, and that her friends were officials from the Ministry of Health studying the distribution of rural health clinics in the state. She hoped that would satisfy his curiosity, but couldn't forgive herself for the security lapse on her part.

An hour or so later, emerging out of the clinic, she found no trace of Samy. Wondering where he might have gone, she ventured into the heart of the village just as some people were seen running out of a house that was in flames. With her medical bag in hand, Su Eng started to run towards the scene, but she didn't get far. Two men surged from nowhere to grab her and dragged her into a house. She struggled to get out of their grip until one of them raised a pistol to her head. She was thoroughly frisked for any weapons on her person. Not finding any, but noticing her concealed ankle holster, they demanded to know where the pistol was.

"I'm an army doctor and don't carry the pistol with me when I visit clinics. I deposited mine at the police station when I came here."

The response was received with a tight slap on her face by the man with the gun, while the other emptied her medical bag onto the floor in search of a hidden weapon. He noticed her name written in medical packaging. He read out aloud her name, and turning round asked her, "You are not a Sabahan, so why are you interfering in our freedom struggle? And where are your comrades?"

Su Eng remained tight-lipped and turned her head away. The man got up and slowly walked up to her. Turning her face around harshly towards him, he drew out his middle finger to touch her lips, and then moved it down slowly towards her throat and onwards to a point mid-way between her breasts. That was as far as he got, for at that instant Su Eng suddenly pushed him forward and kicked him hard in the groin. The man fell flat on the floor at the same time as she felt the butt of a pistol smash into the back of her head. When she came to, she found herself gagged and securely tied up seated in a chair. Her assailants weren't around. She heard the commotion outside the house and realised that must have drawn them away. She struggled to squeeze out of the ropes that tied her hands to the chair, but it was to no avail. She then became conscious of the pain on her head and sensed she was bleeding. She wondered where Samy was. Surely, he would by now know that she was no longer in the clinic. Instinctively, she trusted him to find her. But then, what if he himself had become a victim? The fleeting thought troubled her. From somewhere deep inside, a sob finally gushed out. She didn't bother trying to smother it, but let the tears come, for her thoughts had now drifted to her aging widowed mother and her teenage sibling in Penang. Who would fend for them if anything happened to her life? She managed to pull herself together after a few moments, telling herself that she was in this predicament because she had opted for it. It was part of her scholarship commitment to serve the army for a few years, but she had stayed on as she enjoyed the challenge of combining an outdoor life with her profession.

Meanwhile, Samy after half an hour's idle wait for Su Eng at the clinic had decided to take a stroll towards the beach. The cool breeze was so refreshing that he stood there for quite a while with his eyes closed and a silent prayer on his lips. Coming out of his pseudo-meditation, his gaze soon fell on two speedboats approaching one end of the village, some 150 metres away. He spotted eight men in face masks alighting from the anchored boats and moving into the village. Instinctively, he knew he was witnessing an insurgency raid. Throwing caution to the winds, and with two guns in his hand, he sprinted across the beach towards the boats.

The raiders upon entering the village broke up into two groups, with one group making a beeline to the house of the ketua kampong. They seemed to know its exact location. They barged in with pistols in hand. The ketua was then having a chat with Kamal.

Both were startled by the unexpected intrusion. Kamal counted there were six intruders and knew that engaging them solo in a gun battle was not a tenable proposition. Were they kidnappers, robbers, or insurgents? The question seemed suddenly irrelevant, as Kamal knew he had little choice but to yield to their order to both of them to sit on the floor with their hands folded over their heads. Advancing towards Kamal, they stripped him of his gun, and demanded to know where his companions were. Kamal immediately realised that enemy spies had tracked their entry into Jambongan.

With no answer forthcoming from Kamal, they kicked and rained blows on him as well as on the ketua for indulging Kamal. The insurgents then bound their wrists together, sat them back-to-back, and tied another rope tightly around their chests. Stripping off their shoes, they also bound each of their ankles tightly together, effectively immobilizing them. Then forcing the ketua's family members out of the house, they poured kerosene all over the place. Finally, shouting in unison their battle cry, "*Al-nasraw al-shahāda*", they set the place ablaze and left the scene. Kamal tried to get up, but it proved to be extremely difficult. Frustration rode him hard. The searing heat from the flames and black smoke were getting ever closer to them. A burning splinter from the roof fell near them, and the floor started to burn. Sliding on their buttocks they moved away. The smell of burning hair soon hit their nostrils.

The ketua, in severe pain, was screaming his lungs out for help. Kamal wondered where Samy and Su Eng were. He had told them where he was headed, and something deep inside told him that no flames would hold them back from barging in, sooner or later. He closed his eyes, and for once in his life, fear gripped him. He realized he was facing a terribly painful death, about to be pulled into the afterlife. He heard the ketua reciting the surah *As-Saffat* (no. 37) to relieve the pangs of death. He felt some inner composure upon hearing this, and then suddenly the resolve to survive surged in him. He had to do something drastic. He brought up his tied legs and swinging his knees stretched the legs in the direction of the fire on the floor.

The end of his trousers started to burn, and blisters rose on his legs. The pain was agonising. Finally, the rope at his ankles gave way. He drew his legs in and with a strenuous heave lifted himself along with the bound ketua.

"Quick, where is the nearest water tap?" he asked the ketua.

"In the bathroom on my left," came the choking reply.

Swinging around, Kamal made his way to the bathroom. He was in luck. The bathroom door which was badly scorched was partially open, and there was a swivel water tap a few feet above the bathroom floor. He kicked open the tap to let the flowing water quench the flames creeping up on his pants. It was a difficult manoeuvre, and he slipped. The ketua groaned as he took the brunt of the fall on the hard floor. The fall, however, enabled Kamal to stretch both his legs below the open tap to quench the flames and soothe the burnt skin.

Samy had in the meanwhile reached the speedboats and had immobilized them by putting sand into the fuel tanks. It was then that he saw the burst of flames from the torched house rising into the sky. He suspected immediately that it was an act of arson perpetrated by the intruders. Sensing that there were lives to be possibly saved, he ran to the back of the house. The screams from therein drew him quickly to the smoke-filled front of the house where he was aghast to see Kamal and the man he was tied to lying as inseparable twins on the wet bathroom floor. Samy immediately realised that the duo had just averted a fiery ordeal. The burn marks on their bodies attested to that. He quickly freed them and ushered them out through the back of the house. As this was at the kitchen end, he grabbed two bottles of water for them on the way out.

"Here, take two tablets of these as well with your water," said Samy retrieving a packet of Panadol tablets from his pocket. Both men heeded the advice without a moment's hesitation. Then noticing Kamal was without his boots, Samy quickly went back in to get them. Handing Su Eng's pistol to Kamal, both the pahlawans then went in pursuit of the insurgents.

The villagers had in the meanwhile rushed out of their houses and were helping to douse the flames that were threatening to engulf neighbouring houses. Weaving through the melee, Kamal and Samy had little trouble spotting the insurgents. They were still wearing their masks, and warning the villagers not to hide their enemy. The pahlawns fired at the masked men, killing instantly three of them. Realising they were being shot at by unseen adversaries, the rest of the insurgents started firing randomly into the crowd, wounding several of the villagers, but before long their guns were all silenced. The gunshots had also drawn out the two insurgents who had captured Su Eng. Samy counted five dead bodies. They were sure they had between them targeted all the eight.

The villagers soon drew their attention to one wounded insurgent who was helplessly lying bleeding at the entrance stairs of a house that was ahead of them. Seeing them approach, the man brought his gun to his head and fired. He had been indoctrinated to prefer martyrdom over capture by infidels. That left two more insurgents on the loose. The thought suddenly struck Samy that they might have made their way to the speedboat. He was right. Kamal spotted them on one of the speedboats struggling to get it started. Stealthily they made their way close to the boats from the village side and engaged the insurgents in a shootout. To their dismay, the pahlwans found that a stray bullet had hit the boat's fuel tank; the explosion that followed effectively ended their chase. They rued their missed chance of capturing the raiders alive to wrest information from them.

Both of them then rushed to the clinic in search of Su Eng, but she was nowhere in sight. As the fire had by this time been contained, Samy engaged the villagers in search of her. Before too long, to their huge relief, they saw Su Eng emerging out of a house aided by villagers who had released her from her immobilised position in the chair. She was cradling her head which was bleeding with one hand.

Shock and disbelief registered on her blood-stained face. Kamal and Samy sprinted towards her and escorted her promptly to the clinic for treatment. Kamal and the ketua who had both sustained some second-degree burns were also treated at the clinic with pain-killer medicines and antibiotics additionally sourced from Su Eng's rummaged medical bag. The wounded villagers were likewise brought over for treatment. Listening to Su Eng's narrative, Kamal was sure her assailants had plans to hold her hostage for ransom.

Calling Zain, Samy apprised him of the encounter with the insurgents, and sought his help in contacting SCSC to send their security enforcement team promptly to the scene. A police contingent from Jambongan town soon arrived. With the formalities of reporting dispensed with, the pahlawans took leave of the villagers, and moved northwards, with Kamal intent on completing their planned trip, come what may. They were, however, conscious that they were now clearly on the enemy's radar. They kept as close as possible to the coastline to take in snapshots both with their cell phones and their spy sunglasses, while the boatman, who had chosen to remain in the boat when the attack occurred, was kept busy carefully manoeuvring the boat past dangerous underwater rocks.

Their next port of call was Kampung Limau-Limau, where they alighted briefly to get to know the villagers. They were a friendly lot who came out to greet them. They said their fishing grounds were at both the Paitan Bay and the Sulu Sea. When queried about marauders and jihadist groups, they said they had no experience of any encounters, and appreciated the security protection they had from SCSC. However, they recalled in recent months hearing speedboats going past their village in the dead of night. They were unsure whether they were SCSC patrols or not.

The pahlawans exchanged understanding looks, and soon bid them farewell to continue their surveillance trip of the island. They went past the two horseshoe edges of the island facing the mainland and took several zoom-in pictures before turning past Southwest Bluff towards Kampung Bahanan, another SCSC-protected village, and finally to the school jetty. The whole trip, including the encounter with the insurgents, trip took them over five hours.

Following a late lunch at Jambongan, they bid farewell to their hosts at the estate and left for their hotel in Paitan. A long briefing session with Zain next followed, with Zain seeking further details on their surveillance of the island and their unexpected encounter with the insurgents.

"We managed to find five secluded and less hazardous disembarking points around the island. We think any of these points could be used by insurgents coming in a convoy of three or four boats in the dead of night. We have indicated these on the map that we have just sent you on the encrypted Message app," said Kamal.

"Any guesses where the ten insurgents came from?" asked Zain.

"They could have set off from any of the five secluded points that we mentioned. They must have got wind of our arrival on the island from their informers."

"Quite likely so, as they came in search of you. One thing is clear, Jambongan Island does indeed feature in their plans. Anyway, it was a close shave for all of you. Glad none of you sustained any serious injury. What are your plans for tomorrow?" asked Zain.

"We feel we need to explore the Paitan River a bit to see if it could be used as a quick getaway route to inland areas of Beluran by infiltrators who might use Jambongan Island as a transit point. After that, we shall head for Kudat," replied Kamal.

"Great, but I'm ordering you all to stay back at Paitan and take a complete day's rest before executing your plans," said a worried Zain, ending the conversation.

Zain knew very well that the pahlawans had glossed over their encounter with the insurgents. It must have been a nerve-wracking experience, particularly for Kamal and Su Eng. He was glad that Samy was able to marshal his skills to save them from the jaws of death, and beat the enemy. His ability to sense danger and react quickly to it stood Samy apart from the rest of the pahlawans. The man had a troubled past - two traumas - that only Zain knew about. The first was Samy's witness of his father being killed in a drunken brawl when he was at a young age, and the second of him and his newly-married wife being ambushed while in a car by remnants of a criminal gang dealing in drugs that he had helped to disband. His wife was killed on the spot. He has since then displayed no outward emotions. Anger was the only feeling that satisfied him, it promised relief no matter how temporary. Making others feel pain soothed that anger that made him merciless in dealing with miscreants who crossed his path in his line of duty. Rumours had it that he had personally tracked the ambushers and decimated all of them, although there appear to be no police records to ascertain that. That said, Samy was not a loose gun, and Zain would not have traded him for any other to be in his team for the mission.

CHAPTER 9

*T*he tsunami scares over, a new alert came the next morning with the news from Datuk Azhari at MinDef that CIA had confirmed that Saadam was already in Sabah and had been there for some months.

"You have to catch Saadam alive. I suggest you attend the high-level meeting which has been called for this afternoon at SCSC HQ. You might get some pointers there. They will be expecting you," were Azahari's closing words on the phone.

Zain immediately alerted the pahlawans, and waited impatiently for the morning to end. He knew he was going to have an interesting meeting with Datuk Johari. The questions confronting everyone were how the much-wanted ISIS strongman had set foot in Sabah. They were not to know the answer to this for months to come, but the devilishly simple arrangement that deposited him in Sabah went beyond the radar of the world's most sophisticated intelligence agencies of Interpol, CIA, MI6, and Mossad.

Before he set out for his afternoon appointment with Datuk Johari and Brigadier General Othman at the SCSC headquarters, Zain had an early morning meeting with Sungkiah and her PP1 team. He wanted them to go on a scouting trip to Tawau town and thence to Pulau Sebatik and explore the island's vulnerability to access by land and sea routes by illegal cross-border immigrants.

"Take a slow drive. Walk through some coastal villages along the way, and also around Tawau, before you hit the island. Put your ears to the ground and look for hints of local knowledge about Saadam Elwan. Also, follow up any leads on persons or places there that you have picked up from the phones that you are constantly tracking. Best for you to stay overnight at Tawau. Shall contact you towards evening after my SCSC meeting. *Semoga berjaya* (good luck)," said Zain.

Entering SCSC headquarters around 2.00 p.m., Zain was greeted by a grave-looking Datuk Johari. He was in the company of Brigadier General Othman and SCSC's director of Civil Actions Division, Ronald Kurup, who had flown in from Kota Kinabalu. Entering the boardroom, Zain saw that ACP Rosmah and the directors of several other Divisions of SCSC were already there, including the directors of maritime enforcement and air operations, and the police special force.

"We are not sure where Saadam Elwan is at the moment or how he entered Sabah," began Datuk Johari, laying his cards on the table. He hesitated a moment before continuing, "The Indonesian State Intelligence Agency, BIN, suspects that he has entered Sabah via the Philippines. If that be the case, he could most probably have picked our east coast to sneak in, perhaps in disguise."

"He is a tall person, according to his profile photo. Whatever his disguise, he is not likely to trim his beard and throw off his white head scarf, as these are in sync with the dress code of the Wahhabis. I bet he is going to wear minimal latex prosthetic pieces on his face. We can easily come up with a set of sketches that might land a match. I further suspect that he might pose as an Arab businessman and lodge himself in some corporate office in town," observed Rosmah.

"You have a valid point. It would be useful to get your sketch artist to quickly come up with some images. I could use them. But his safety is going to depend on his quick mobility around the state. He will become an easy target, otherwise, if he remains in the one place," noted Zain.

"We have received offers of help from the CIA in tracking him down here, but MinDef is treating their offer on hold, as it is still smarting over recent damning statements in the Western press that Muslims in Malaysia *are slowly but surely becoming radicalized.*" The observation appears to have been based on the reported detection by Bukit Aman on social media of a few Malaysians heading to Syria and the southern Philippines to partake in their jihad for an Islamic State. We have no positive evidence from our locals about his presence in Sabah, but if he is just planning to arrive, he might postpone his entry or even abort it in the face of advance national publicity," said Datuk Johari.

"But what if he is already here as has been claimed by CIA?. How long does MinDef plan to withhold this information from the public?" asked the director of maritime enforcement, whose countenance revealed that he disliked the idea altogether. "Religious conservatism is one thing, but these guys have carried orthodoxy to extreme levels that are barbaric in my eyes. Look at the genocide they perpetrated on the Yazidis. They are unquestionably a narcissistic and solipsistic lot. Once they get a foothold here, they will similarly start exterminating some of our indigenous Muslims who have not shed their tribal customs, much like the *kejawen* in Indonesia." His words dripped disgust for the militant religious zealots.

"There is no point alarming the public unless we have proof that an ISIS strongman has set foot in the state. All entry points to Sabah and the rest of Malaysia, however, have been placed on alert," responded Othman.

"But just last night, I heard on Al Jazeera that our country is already on high alert for a top-level ISIS intrusion." The new voice was that of the director of air operations.

"Good gracious! The leakage must have come from our immigration, probably through a freelance defence journalist. But I'm sure MinDef will deny the high alert report if they are ever queried by our local reporters. It's a cause for immense worry all the same, whether he is about to set foot or is already here," noted Othman.

"The notion of an Islamic State will gain greater momentum if ISIS gains a foothold in our country and propagate their brand of Islam, which preaches a brutal form of Syariah law. Corrupt and ambitious politicians and armed personnel will be used as pawns in their schemes. I have seen that happen before," warned Zain.

"What exactly will be his role in coming to Sabah to help rewind history and bring back the Sulu sultanate, and along with it establish an Islamic State, all in one go?" asked another member of the audience.

"Precisely! But this can only be achieved by wide-scale militancy and terrorism. So, it will be a long-term objective. His immediate objective, I suspect, will be to set up terror cells and convert more people to their cause from within Sabah and from neighbouring Mindanao and Kalimantan, who will form the backbone of strong militant separatist movements. The final, overarching objective is to convert the three regions into Islamic States. They intend this to be their new extremist zone as ISIS loses its territories in the Middle East. We have to nab our man at all costs," said Datuk Johari.

Rosmah spoke: "Yes, we have to nip his plans in the bud. The crackdown on extremist groups by the new Philippine government has been severe in Mindanao, where one in five residents is Muslim. We have learnt that the backbone of the Abu Sayyaff group has been broken, and many of them have either been captured or fled to Sabah. However, a new terror group has in recent months captured the jihad mantle of the Islamic State. This is the group that calls itself the Bangsamoro Islamic Freedom Fighters. Remnants of the Abu Sayaff have also joined them."

"Looks like we need to place more of our spies on the ground here, as well as in Mindanao," said Zain, smiling and looking at Rosmah.

Rosmah was quick to respond. "I think ASP Zain has a point. From the police angle here, we have to have more checkpoints on the roads, and also on the inland waterways."

"There is a need also, I think, to monitor their funding source. This means tracking local bank transactions involving foreign funds and heavy local deposits," noted Zain.

"Money laundering is already a brisk business here in Sabah. How exactly can we proceed to connect it with our wanted man?" asked Ronald Kurup.

"We certainly would need to seek the help of both Bank Negara and the Malaysian Anti-Corruption Commission. The branches of both local and foreign banks here in Sabah and Labuan will have to be thoroughly investigated in a blitz operation for non-resident accounts and accounts held by companies registered in Hong Kong, the UK, and elsewhere, arising from illegal dealings in timber and gold," responded Zain.

"We also have to see who the owners of the banks are. I have been reading reports of banks that had gone bust in the USA but are still holding majority shares in some European banks," chipped in Kurup.

"You may be right. It is possible to happen here as well. We cannot also ignore the possibility that some of such money may be used to buy political influence, and also to fund terror cells," replied Zain.

"There is little doubt we have to explore all angles and enhance both our vigil and surveillance. Concerning our maritime surveillance, ASP Zain has asked me whether we can manoeuvre our ships to the edge of international limit closest to some neighbouring islands to spy on activities there using drones. He feels that for clandestine entry in large numbers, some of such islands may serve as embarking points for the Bangsamoro Islamic Freedom Fighters and remnants of other previous militant groups that have joined them," said Datuk Johari.

"Yes, we are looking for evidence in the form of new harbour constructions and sudden increases in the number of speedboats and tugboats. Conceivably, we can create the scene of one of our patrol boats chasing a decoy speedboat, wherein we have our men posing as kidnappers, and send a drone ahead towards the decoy boat that quickly flies around the island as well. Can't we?" asked Zain.

The director of maritime enforcement took up the challenge to respond. "It is all the same a frivolous act, and presumes that there is no vigilance by the Filipino authorities on the island. It is also an act that cannot be repeated without arousing suspicion. We have recently proposed to MinDef to initiate a trilateral maritime patrol involving counterparts from Indonesia and the Philippines to cover the expanse of the Sulu Sea, especially around Sabah's hot spot tourist destinations."

"Does the joint patrol include the sea environment around Taganak and Sibutu?" asked Zain.

"Not particularly. Our focus essentially is to reduce the incidence of kidnapping and smuggling, and to provide a safety net for tourists who love our isolated island paradises. For a start, we have identified the sea around only three islands – Mantanani Island, which is a cluster of three isolated tiny islands to the northwest of Kota Belud noted for scuba diving; Lankayan Island, which also boasts a turtle rehabilitation centre; and Mabul Island, which is one of the world's top-rated destinations for muck diving," replied the director.

"I'm sure, if need be, a bilateral maritime patrol can be explored for other security-sensitive areas, following this start. Thank you all for your views and suggestions on how we need to beef up our security. The news of the presence of the ISIS strongman in our state can but only add a sense of urgency to our efforts, both for his capture and for eliminating all fomented terror acts," said Datuk Johari, by way of a concluding remark that ended the meeting.

Returning from the SCSC meeting, Zain immediately contacted Sungkiah for any snippets of information that she and her team may have gathered, while apprising them about his meeting. There appeared to be a wall of silence surrounding the ISIS strongman. An indirect hint, however, came their way when Sungkiah and her team decided out of the blue to have their lunch break at an Arab restaurant.

It all began, according to Sungkiah, halfway through their lunch, when they noticed that a scuffle had broken out at the kitchen end of the restaurant between two parties. A sturdy-looking man in an all-black attire who was seated alone at a table near the entrance took flight at the scene, carrying with him onto the road two rucksacks. Because of the hullabaloo, no one had noticed his departure, save for Sungkiah, who was seated across the aisle from the man. Suspicious about the man's sudden exit, Sungkiah followed him on foot past two roads and saw him going into an open staircase entrance of a double-storey shop lot. She waited by the roadside, watching the shop's side entrance. A car rolled up within the hour, and two persons escorting a third alighted from it. The car then sped away.

The escorted person was a foreigner, a white male. Sungkiah walked along the opposite side of the road to the shop and saw one of the bodyguards was stationed at the shop's side entrance. Nonchalantly walking towards him, Sungkiah showed him a piece of paper as if to ascertain an address, and in a swift movement, knocked him out. Laying him at the foot of the stairs, she quietly climbed up to the upper floor, wearing her headgear and spy sunglasses. There were six people in the room. She saw the man with the two rucksacks unloading bundles of money in US dollars and several gold bars onto a table. She waited a moment to learn what the transaction was all all about.

"There was some argument in the restaurant as to whether or not I should be additionally given the gold bars because of the shortfall of cash brought in by the money changers. I left the place unseen as soon as a fight broke out," said the man who had brought in the rucksacks, while peeling off his facial mask

"It's clever of you to go in disguise. Hopefully you were not followed here, and they don't know about this place," said the foreigner wearing a wry smile on his lips. He paused to get affirmation, and then continued. "What you have placed before me will get you a couple of dozen M-16 assault rifles and almost all the precursor materials in this list for making PIEDs and VIEDs (person-borne and vehicle-borne improvised explosive devices). We leave it to you to source only for urea and sawdust yourselves, if you need them at all later. You have to be careful in handling and storing the nitric acid, hydrogen peroxide, and the perchlorate salts. But, of course, you people are experts at this. You need to give us three weeks to organise all these, and I shall contact you when ready for instructions where exactly you want them delivered."

Sungkiah sensed that she was with a mixed group of sleeper agents and money launderers who may be connected with Saadam. Bursting upon them in the room would be a foolhardy action, a lost opportunity to nail them to a terror cell that was in the making. She had to tail them. She quickly descended the stairs and removed from the still unconscious bodyguard his wrist watch and wallet, to give the impression of a street robbery. She then messaged Azlan to come with Dhanyal to keep a tight vigil on the place and take turns to follow individuals coming out of the shop lot.

Reflecting on the information received from Sungkiah, Zain was sure that Saadam was already in the country, and that organising IEDs would certainly be a first act on his agenda. It was also clear to him that terror cells for the training of recruits in wielding firearms would have to be situated in remote inland areas, accessible perhaps only by riverine transport. He looked at a spread-out map of Tawau Division. His fingers followed its boundaries westward to the Interior Division and southwards to Kalimantan. That was a lot of territory that could hide innumerable terror cells. The simplest solution that struck him was one of phone tapping suspected sympathisers and the discreet monitoring of middlemen involved in supplying food and other materials to inland areas. He hoped that more revelations would be forthcoming from the pahlawans.

Putting his phone on the speaker mode, he spoke to Sungkiah and her mates.

"Do carry on with your trip to Pulau Sebatik tomorrow. Perhaps we may get some pointers there about Saadam. I suspect he is already in our midst, and that means his signature IEDs will soon be on a shattering display. I'm hazarding a guess that for maximal terror impact, the IEDs would probably be first used in Kota Kinabalu, Sandakan, and Lahad Datu. We have to be on the lookout for their likely targets in these towns and advise the authorities accordingly to have surveillance cameras emplaced there, wherever possible. How and when the attacks will take place is anybody's guess. The way they have gone about their tasks in UK and France is an indication of things to come on our shores. More than ever, you have to broaden your efforts at phone tapping. Get in touch also with Nasri Abdurajak. We may be able to use him for trailing purposes. And, oh, I plan to head for Sandakan tomorrow. There is a phone lead that has landed on my plate. I need to check it out."

Zain's phone lead had come from Datuk Azhari in MinDef.

"We have come to know that our fugitive, Mario, is in Sandakan. The police warrant for his arrest has not materialised yet. He was probably in his homeland until now. There was apparently a computer alert on him at the Sandakan jetty immigration as he crossed into Sabah with a new passport about two weeks ago, but they allowed him in as the name on his passport was different, and there was also some aberration with his thumb print. You may want to track him down there personally."

Zain needed no second invitation, for he had a score to settle with Mario. His presence in Sabah coinciding with the arrival of Saadam also forebode a period of turmoil soon in the state which Zain was committed to negate at all costs.

CHAPTER 10

*T*he 175-kilometre trip from Lahad Datu to Sandakan took Zain slightly more than three hours, as the police had checkpoints installed along various stretches of the road. He headed straight to Ghosthouse upon arrival, breaking only for lunch along a road stretch. The long drive had given him ample time to dwell on issues that needed to be confronted to meet the underground network of terror that was being established. Against that, the present threat of 'hit and run' sea incursions on the state's east coast would only be a trifling matter to contend with. The enormity of the challenge, he was sure, was not being fully realised by the state government machinery. He knew that security was a federal government matter, and both the country's Home Affairs and Defence Ministries had to be intimated. He toyed with the idea of taking a flight back to Kuala Lumpur to meet up with General Ghazali Abu Hassan. He called Datuk Azhari to discuss the matter first, but was told that the general was overseas and would be back in a week. He then made an appointment to meet up with the Sandakan police chief, Assistant Commissioner Mohd. Arshad.

It was a long meeting that Zain had with Arshad. They examined together with markings on the map the most likely riverine sites for cargo loading and transport of food supplies to inland areas in the Sandakan and Beluran Divisions of the state, and the possibility of police patrols in these areas. Zain also got from Arshad a listing of all banks operating in Sandakan, and the names and contact numbers of the bank managers. Arshad, of course, queried him on this need, but Zain explained it away thus:

"Money laundering, as you know, is often through the medium of banks. While all banks are obliged to have internal mechanisms in place for monitoring and reporting fraudulent or even suspicious transactions involving large intra-or inter-transfer of funds between accounts, there have been clear lapses in their vigilance. In some cases, this has been traced to rogue employees in the banks. Money laundering and terrorism funding is very much on our minds these days."

Zain had barely reached Ghosthouse after the meeting when he received a call from Arshad. A bomb blast had occurred at the Thirsty Gulp Pub at the Grand Concorde Hotel overlooking Sandakan Bay, a favourite haunt of tourists. The blast, which occurred at around 7.00 p.m., had claimed four lives, and many had incurred severe injuries.

Video clippings of the sanguinary incident soon started to go viral in the social media, and a news ticker on a national television channel showed ISIS had claimed credit for the incident. Zain quickly descended on the scene and surmised that it was a case of a PIED. Meeting Arshad

126

there, he whispered, "Looks like Saadam has signalled his arrival in Sabah. I suspect he must have landed here first a few months back; this blast is his handiwork. He could be anywhere now." The mutilated body of the suicide bomber was being isolated by the forensics team that had arrived, but it was clear to Zain that it was a small-sized bomb and the carrier was a local.

"We are examining the undamaged CCTV cameras leading to the pub area," said Arshad.

"No doubt it will only confirm that he came alone to the hotel without an accomplice. He would have entered by a back entrance. I'm suspecting that the IED was fabricated in a shop lot or residential town building, and the jihadist was dropped at least 100 metres or more from the hotel by a vehicle. If there are CCTV cameras at the rear of the hotel and along the road stretch leading to the hotel, these may need to be looked at," opined Zain to a nodding Arshad.

Upon his return to Ghosthouse, Zain contacted Kamal to hear about his team's trip upstream in the Paitan River and into areas of the Kudat Division. They mentioned going past Kampong Paitan up to the road bridge of the Sapi-Nangoh Highway. The villagers, called orang sungai, living along the banks pursued a nomadic boat lifestyle with their livelihood based almost exclusively on fishing. The pahlawans concluded that the lower reaches of the river were more suited for infiltrators to make a fast getaway. Their conclusion about Kudat was that the

Division could not be sustained as a potential enemy stronghold on logistics grounds, and also because of the tight SCSC security net around its entire coastline.

"Where are you presently?" asked Zain of Kamal.

"On the return leg to Sandakan. We're near Pitas and will spend the night there. We just heard about the blast," replied Kamal.

"Probably the right thing to do. A curfew has already been imposed on a 10-kilometre radius from the Grand Concorde Hotel, which takes in the bulk of the residential areas to the north and west of the hotel, with house-to-house searches by the police for Saadam Elwan. Not sure when they will lift the curfew. Luckily, our Ghosthouse is outside the curfew perimeter area. See you guys in the morning," replied Zain, walking towards his bedside to charge his phone.

Lying in bed, Zain scanned the named list of banks operating in Sandakan that Arshad had furnished him. He recalled that some of them had previously been taken to task by the country's Central Bank for not reporting money laundering evidence in their hands. However, his eyes soon settled on two banks which he knew had foreign bank shareholdings. His restless mind demanded getting a full disclosure of all non-resident accounts they held. He knew this was not going to be possible without the mediation of the Central Bank, unless he was able to secure the services of bank insiders.

Acting on an impulse, he unplugged his phone from its charger and sourced for information on the monitoring process adopted by banks for suspicious transactions. This led him to the workings of one of the largest banks in Southeast Asia, which also had a branch in Sandakan. He was surprised to learn that the tracking process used by the bank was not a tedious one, but rather a simple one-minute affair using technologies that leverage artificial intelligence to conduct investigative research on both individuals and companies suspected of illegal financing. He wondered whether all other banks adopted similar technologies.

For a start, he would be contended with police help, if that was possible, to receive information from all the banks in Sandakan of the most active new accounts over the last six months.

Upon the arrival of the PP2 team, Zain entered into a brainstorming session with them.

"Let's discuss the most plausible landing or transit points on Pulau Jambongan that you have identified," began Zain, laying out a blown-up map of Beluran on the table.

"The most likely spot they might head for on the island would be Kampung Nibong, we think," said Kamal, marking the approximate position of the site on the map. He went on to add, "This would be the case if they have confiscated boats of local fishermen at sea for their entry into the island. We have tapped the ketua kampung's phone there. Hopefully, we can get a lead by listening in, but I have found that the reception is very poor."

"Paitan River is the river the terrorists would most likely use to make a quick getaway into the mainland from Pulau Jambongan. However, there are a lot of other small streams that flow into Paitan Bay that they can access for temporary refuge in case their boats are spotted," noted Su Eng.

"The key question is, where would their final destinations be once they reached the Belarus mainland? I'm sure that without the local support of sympathisers, they will not get far. Even so, their terror cells cannot be deep in, as they are intended for training recruits and sending them out. They are not likely to engage in anything like the guerrilla-type warfare we witnessed during the Communist occupation of Peninsular Malaysia. Their tactics will be one of sabotage, fuelling fear and unrest, and whipping up local sentiments for an Islamic State," observed Samy.

At that moment, Zain received a call from Sungkiah. He immediately placed his phone on speaker mode so that all of them could listen in to the conversation.

"We tailed the white foreigner and his two companions to Kunak after their meeting in Tawau. They checked in at a hotel there overnight, and were seen visiting a few shops in the Chinese sector of the town the next day, including a visit to the TML Remittance centre. We followed them also to the jetty, which was some five kilometres from the town. We saw them talking to a few boatmen who had arrived there. His registered name in the hotel was Anton, and I have sent you by secure mail his photograph and that of his car. This morning he has taken the road north, presumably heading your way,"

Zain's face lit up at this news. "That's splendid work! Anton is our best lead so far into the militant network. We shall seek police assistance to inform us about the arrival and location of the car here, and then put a tail on him. I shall, in the meanwhile, persuade Brigadier General Othman to try and weed out information on the nature of Anton's transaction at the TML Remittance centre."

"Wasn't Kunak in the news recently? I remember reading about several people there, including a police corporal, being arrested on suspicion of aiding Suluk terrorists," asked Su Eng.

"Yes. The police seized from them sharp weapons, membership cards, appointment letters, and documents linked to the Sulu sultanate," recalled Zain.

Zain then called Arshad, seeking the latter's help in notifying him of the whereabouts of Anton's car that was coming into Sandakan past the police roadblocks along the way.

"No issues. The curfew has just been lifted. Will notify you when the car gets on our radar. By the way, the suicide bomber has been identified as a former member of the Jemaah Islamiyah militant group in Indonesia," responded Arshad.

"That's interesting. This tells me that Saadam's recruitment of local militia has already commenced. I have a feeling they may stage another attack soon," replied Zain.

"Oh, what makes you say that?"

"From what I have read, they rarely send out just the one suicide bomber. Very often it's a pair, either to the same destination or different destinations."

"How does one pick out these guys in the open?"

"For a start, I would stop and check all pedestrians walking about town with large backpacks. And, I hate saying this, but there's a tendency among our police not to check those who wear turbans and dress up in robes traditionally worn by religious scholars. They feel that would be an insulting act. If you ask me, there should be no discrimination when it comes to checking. An M-16 assault rifle can easily be hidden under a robe."

"I see your point. Illegals may have entered our shores using this tactic to avoid detection. I shall have to bring this to the notice of security at roadblocks and immigration points. But you have got me worried about the second attack."

"If I can be of any help, I can come over right away with some of my team members to discuss the matter with you. I also need to seek your help in locating a person who has escaped my clutches in the past. I'm told he has turned up recently in Sandakan."

"Sure thing. Please come straight to my office."

With a thumbs-up sign, Zain beckoned Kamal to accompany him for the meeting with Arshad before he left to join Samy in tailing Anton once the latter arrived in town.

Turning next to Su Eng, he said, "I need you here for some solid electronic trailing work. We haven't a clue yet on the likely locations of the dens of the militants. Please liaise with PP1 who are still in Tawau to sort out all the intercepted messages gleaned to date from their phones. Perhaps some new leads might emerge."

Arshad cordially greeted Zain and Kamal, and they went straight into discussing the overall security problem that was confronting the state. Also present at the meeting was the municipal council chairman. They looked intently at a street map of Sandakan and highlighted on it places where people might tend to congregate in large numbers.

Suddenly, Kamal was seized with an alarming thought.   "What if they are waiting for a specific occasion, like a regional conference or....." Kamal let the word hang in the air.

"Or what?" asked Arshad.

"I was thinking of the last day of Tadau Kaamatan, the Kadazan-Dusun harvest festival, which is about a week away. The last day often attracts large crowds," muttered Kamal.

"Yes, they may well choose that time to instil further fear and unrest in the town," observed Arshad, hastily encircling the area on the map with his marker pen.

Zain concurred, and they spent a good half-hour brainstorming on the precautions to be taken.

"Perhaps we should confine all planned performances associated with the festival to defined areas of the town, the entry to which will be unidirectional from a given street. That way, you can screen all those intending to watch the events as they proceed past the barricades. There has to be surveillance cameras also installed at strategic points." The words came from the municipal council chairman.

"That's a good idea, although it might inconvenience the public and make them unduly anxious. Perhaps even the attendance might suffer," commented Zain.

"Well, we need to consider all angles," concluded Arshad.

"Why don't you discuss the matter with the Sabah Tourism Board and get back to me?"

"Will do," replied the council chairman, who then took his leave.

As soon as the man had left, Zain handed Arshad a photograph.

"Is this individual, by any chance, in your police records?"

It was the picture of Mario. Arshad immediately summoned an officer to look into the computer records and to report back. Simultaneously, his office phone buzzed. He turned to Zain.

"Your car has been spotted entering Leila Road."

That was the signal for Kamal to leave the meeting and join up with Samy. Left alone with Arshad, Zain confided in him of his interest in Mario

Dancers in traditional attire performing the Sumazau during Tadau Kaamatan
(Photo credit: kdca.org.my, via Amazing Borneo Tours)

"Old habits die hard. If Mario is here for establishing a clandestine gun manufacturing facility, he will

135

probably deal again with a local Chinese industrial engineering company with an import licence for machinery parts from overseas. I'm afraid I have to seek your assistance again to get me a few names that might fit the bill in the Sandakan area as soon as possible."

Arshad smiled. "Shouldn't be too difficult. But let's break for some early lunch, shall we?"

When they came back, they got the news that the police did not have Mario in their files, but there was a ready list of engineering companies that Zain could investigate. As he left the police station, there was a call on his mobile from Brigadier General Othman, confirming that a P2B (individual to business) transaction was conducted by Anton at the TML Remittance in Kunak to a business entity in Davao, Mindanao.

Meanwhile, in downtown Sandakan, Samy and Kamal spotted Anton as he and his henchmen alighted from their car in a parking lot along Leila Road. One of his bodyguards was wielding a bag. Kamal followed them at a distance as the trio walked cautiously towards a goldsmith's shop, while Samy went towards the car to hide a GPS tracking chip.

There was a security guard seated outside the building who looked lost to the world. With Kamal remaining outside pretending to read messages on his phone, Samy entered the shop. He saw Anton waiting for the manager and then both of them retreating into an inner room, with Anton now carrying the bag. Samy stayed on in the pretext of looking for a pendant with a religious motif, and positioned himself on the stool away from the line of sight of Anton the moment he saw him come out of the manager's room. With the departure of Anton and his bodyguards, Kamal entered the shop, and with Samy at his side went straight to the manager. Parading a gun in his hand, Kamal presented his credentials as an SCSC officer.

"Have you met the man who walked in here before? What's in the bag that he brought in?" asked Kamal of the manager.

"No, sir, I haven't seen him before. But I received a call from the chief of my security firm to expect him. He had some gold bars that he wanted to sell. He wanted cash. I told him to come back tomorrow," came the prompt reply.

Kamal then demanded that the CCTV footage be handed to him immediately, and promised the manager a hefty fine, closure of his business, and years in jail for money laundering if he did not play along and extend his cooperation in catching Anton. Kamal then made an audio recording of the manager confirming receipt of seven 1kg gold bars for sale from Anton at the agreed price.

"You will act normally and give him the agreed sum when he comes in tomorrow. You will, in the meanwhile, hold these gold bars and the cash receipt from Anton in your possession until further notice. They may be used as evidence. And, by the way, write down for me the name and contact number of the chief of your security firm. We will meet again, and remember what I told you."

Kamal and Samy then left the shop to get back to Ghosthouse, leaving the manager in a daze.

Back at Ghosthouse, Kamal and the pahlawans diligently sifted through the intercepted conversations and messages recorded on their phones, looking for anything out of the ordinary. They were not concerned with coded messages – they didn't expect any, as they were not dealing with trained spies, but rather ordinary people who had been roped in by militants as sympathisers or paid informers. As was to be expected, the language they had to contend with was largely local, which turned out to be a potpourri of dialects. Translated, the following recurring words stood out, which in their estimation could have a bearing on either criminal or militant activities: *boat rental, shelter, interior village, recruits, second-hand cars, friendly police, supplies, night market, government office, check points, coast guards, fake passports, Pulau Jambongan, Pulau Sebatik, Tawau, Kinabatangan, Sungai-Sungai, Sandakan, Tanjung Labian, Kunak.*

Conspicuously absent was any reference to a particular timeline or date, gun or detonator, or even the word *jihad.* The intercepted messages gave no hint of any imminent threat or its nature; perhaps the perpetrators didn't want to share that information outside of their inner circle. The solution appeared to be either tailing a potential recruit or an intimate contact to their hidden camps or penetrating their fold in either of those capacities. They had more or less resigned to this conclusion, when out of the blue, Kamal received a call from Sungkiah.

"Hi, this is pahlawan Sungkiah. I received a call a few moments ago from Nasri Abdurajak. I'm sending you herewith his audio message. Please also inform the boss about it. I couldn't reach him just now."

They all listened intently to the message. "Hello, everyone, Nyamuk here. The cartel group was here yesterday and were looking for able-bodied men to be recruited as bodyguards. A monthly salary of one thousand ringgits was quoted. They said that those selected will be taken away for training in martial arts and the use of firearms at special centres. In all, over twenty youths were interviewed and they selected a dozen of them, including my cousin. Families of those selected were given five hundred ringgits each for agreeing to release them. They then left, saying that they would come for the selected men in two days."

Zain reacted quickly upon hearing the news. It struck him as a clear case of militant recruitment. He instructed Sungkiah to contact Nasri immediately.

"Tell him to meet up with you today. I want you to purchase a new cell phone, install in it the Flexi spyware, and ask Nasri to present it as his gift to his cousin. No telling what information we may be able to extract from it. You can confide to Nasri about the phone's spy tracking capability. Can you manage that?"

"Consider it done!" came Sungkiah's reply. "And one more piece of news, sir. Nasri overheard the cartel group mentioning Sukau a couple of times. I looked it up. It's on the Kinabatangan River. Perhaps they have a hidden camp there."

"It's probable. Seems to me we may have to visit the place soon. If Nasri has discreetly taken a photograph of these people, get him to send it to you."

"Yes, sir," replied Sungkiah.

CHAPTER 11

*T*he Singapore Airlines flight that touched down at Kota Kinabalu International Airport at 7.05 p.m. was spot on time. Among its passengers were two undercover CIA agents, with false diplomatic passports showing their attachment to the US Embassy in Bangkok. Singapore was just their transit point. Fluent in both Arabic and Indonesian, they were first sent from their station in Libya, where they were heavily involved in intelligence gathering work, to Thailand to investigate growing anti-US sentiment there. Their presence in Sabah was a new assignment – that of tracking the whereabouts of the newly-arrived ISIS jihadi leader, Saadam Elwan. However, to all and sundry they were just tourists taking a break from their Bangkok embassy to experience the delights of Sabah's marvellous undersea coral reefs and lowland forests.

Arriving at the registration desk at their hotel, they received a written message to call a local number. The response was immediate.

"Welcome to Sabah. We have booked you both in adjacent rooms with an interconnecting door. The waiter that is going to bring you a welcome drink will discreetly hand you a locked bag. The code to open it is 9-1-1. Good luck on your mission." The phone then went dead.

They wasted no time in entering their respective rooms. As soon as the waiter had left them, they hurriedly opened the bag to reveal a letter along with a few items. Opening the letter, they read:

"You will find in this bag two Glock 40-calibre revolvers, a sealed pack of ammunition (100 rounds), two local SIM cards, and a bunch of car keys bearing the car registration number. It's a Land Rover camper vehicle which is parked in the hotel parking lot. The security here is presently very tight. Make sure you're not caught with the weapons in your possession by the local authorities. Along with the car keys, I have attached a key to a locker, rented under the name of a fictitious company, at the Tanjung Aru railway station here in Kota Kinabalu. You are expected to leave your weapons inside the locker once you leave these shores. Just message your exit to the number given to you at the hotel desk when you are done. Good luck again on your mission."

Anton felt a bit uneasy after collecting the money from the goldsmith's shop the next day at mid-morning. He had seen a definite change on the manager's face, and the man's rather brisk attendance on him suggested that something odd was afoot. Heading towards his car, he wondered whether the bag he was carrying contained marked currency notes. Suddenly, he stopped. Acting on his sixth sense, he rushed back alone to the shop and redeposited the bag with the manager.

"Look, I cannot carry this money bag with me where I'm going just now. It's safer with you. I shall collect it tomorrow. On second thoughts, I have also decided that I don't want the payment in ringgits. Please give me the equivalent in US dollars." Without waiting for a reply, Anton then left the manager.

Samy, witnessing Anton's antics from his car, knew at once that the man was already suspicious. He saw Anton speaking on his mobile as he stepped out of the shop with no bag in his hands, lingering there for a few moments, and then entering his car as it was driven to him. The car then sped off. Samy quickly notified Kamal, who was at Ghosthouse, of the happenings, and he continued to tail the car at a distance.

It was a couple of hours later that Kamal arrived at the shop in a taxi. He was surprised to see police cars there. He approached a bystander who told him that a robbery and kidnapping had taken place. "The salesgirl in the shop told me that two men wearing masks and waving guns in the air had entered the shop from a black sedan that parked itself in front of the shop. They broke the display boxes and grabbed as much jewellery as they could, and then entered the manager's room. They beat up the manger as he was trying to alert the police, took a bagful of money that was on his table, and also kidnapped the guy. It took the police twenty minutes to arrive."

Meanwhile, Anton, feeling secure that he was not being followed after an hour on the drive, sent a missed call to one of his henchmen. The response was immediate.

"Boss, we have got back the money bag along with plenty of jewellery. We also have with us the rat who tipped the police. We have thrown away his phone as you directed."

"Good. Hope you are not being followed. Take him to our house, and tie him up, gagged, in one of the rooms. Guard him well until I arrive. Hide the money and jewellery in the usual place under the kitchen floor. You have to get rid of the black sedan that you stole for the job as soon as possible. There is a shopping mall nearby with a covered carpark. I want one of you to take the car and leave it there. But do it at the office rush hour. Send me an alarm signal if you sense any trouble."

Back at Ghosthouse, Zain, upon hearing the news from Kamal, suspected that Anton might have staged the robbery and kidnapping using his own bodyguards, and that the purpose was also to send a warning message to those on his tail. He immediately contacted Samy and apprised him of the events.

"Look, I want you to kidnap Anton from his car at the first opportunity and take him, blindfolded, to our Ghosthouse. I'm sure he would have instructed his bodyguards where to hide the goldsmith. Squeeze out the information from him if he doesn't respond to the normal interrogation."

"With great pleasure," responded Samy with no small amount of glee.

Late that afternoon saw Anton being unceremoniously bundled into Ghosthouse for a quick punch bag workout by Samy. Falling to his knees with his face bleeding and puffed up in pain, Anton spilled out the answers to questions that were shot at him.

"We know you are trading in illegal firearms. Who are your suppliers, and for whom are they intended? Where have you taken the goldsmith?" These were the first questions hurled at him. The answers came in a torrent, as the man was terrified.

"I get the weapons mostly from Mindanao, brought on a trailer which comes near Kunak. They are then unloaded onto fishing boats. We have a number of fishermen on our pay who bring them unnoticed to their kampung homes from where we collect them and bring them over to my house here. I really do not know my clients but only their middlemen, who pay me in advance and then later collect the firearms from my house when they become available. Only sometimes I deliver them to where they want."

Zain, who had by then arrived at the Ghosthouse, and was audio-recording Anton's statement, interrupted to ask, "What's the address of your house? Name us also the places where you were asked to deliver the firearms." The man answered without hesitation.

"Are you a citizen of Sabah?"

"No, sir, only a permanent resident. I'm originally from Lebanon. My wife is a Kadazan."

"Let me see your passport."

"It's in my bag in the car, sir."

"Where does your wife live? Give me the particulars. By the way, are you aware of the presence of an ISIS jihadist in our midst?"

"No, sir," replied Anton, while writing the information sought about his wife on a piece of paper that had been handed to him.

"You handle guns, but do you know how to use them?"

"Yes, sir."

"What about PIEDs?"

"I only know the materials, but do not know how to assemble them."

"Look, if you are caught by the police, you will immediately be slapped with the charges of gunrunning, money laundering, kidnapping, and abetting militants. This will land you the death sentence, as per our laws. We are part of an undercover national security team and have a choice on our hands — to hand you over to the police for a direct trip to hell or rope you in to work for us to track down the terror cells in the state. What say you?"

Anton was bewildered for a moment before he replied, "Spare me, sir. I shall work for you. I shall be loyal. I swear."

"You'd better be. We shall not hesitate to eliminate you if you betray us or try to sneak out of the country. Your passport will be kept by us for safe custody. And how exactly do you think you can help us?"

"I can identify the people who contact me for the firearms, and find out where they are being sent."

"Good. How do you despatch the supplies to your clients?"

"I pack them after their inspection in boxes or large backpacks before they take hold of them."

Zain welcomed the information, as the boxes and backpacks could be tagged to determine their ultimate location.

"Good. From now on, every time you engage in packing, some of us will be there to assist. When are you next expecting receipt of your order of weapons in Kunak?" asked Zain.

"In about a month, sir."

"By the way, are your bodyguards locals?"

"Yes, sir."

"All right, but don't breathe a word to them about your connection with us. Introduce us as your new friends and say we saved you from being robbed by a gang on the highway. Here's your phone. Call them now and order them to take the goldsmith, blindfolded, away from the house, along with all the stolen jewellery and leave him safely at some park entrance. And say you will meet up with them later in the evening."

Zain then took the phone away from Anton and passed it to Samy with an understanding wink to install the Flexispy software on it.

CHAPTER 12

*I*t was a different batch of men that came to Kampung
Kerinchi the following day to fetch the identified recruits.
They had brought along a painted-over school bus, into
which they seated the recruits. The recruits were all
provided with caps and hiking boots. Nasri coaxed them all
to pose for a group photograph before they left. He also
noted the registration number of the vehicle, although he
knew it could well be false. As soon as the vehicle was out
of sight, he transmitted the information to Sungkiah.

The school bus headed towards Hills Park, a 280-
square-kilometres protected rainforest known to boast
some of the tallest tropical trees in the world. The bus
dropped the recruits at the park entrance and left them in
the hands of an assigned park ranger. They were treated to
a simple hot meal of noodles and teh tarik in the office
canteen. Following this, they were told they would be going
on a hilly hike through the forest towards Gunung (Mount)
Lucia.

"You will encounter all types of wildlife along the
way, especially the long-tailed Macaques, *musang* (wild cats),
and hornbills. Do not disturb them. Be careful when you
are passing the *mengaris* tees; the bees like to make their

hives there. So, if we are all ready, let's move," said the ranger.

Halfway up their trek, they were met by a band of three persons in jungle-green outfits carrying rifles who appeared suddenly on the scene from behind a thick vegetation cover. The ranger paused as he saw them. He went over to have a brief dialogue with the leader of the band, and then indicated to the startled recruits that these men would now lead them on the final leg of their journey. He then took their leave to head back to the park office.

"We shall walk on for a short distance more along this track, and then we will veer off it towards our hidden training camp, where you will be provided your basic training. We shall be staying at the camp for a few weeks before we move out elsewhere. At this point, I want all of you to hand me your phones," said the rugged-looking leader of the band.

The recruits, who were somewhat awed, wore apprehensive looks, not knowing what they had walked into. They trudged on for an hour or so more, up and down the undulating terrain that virtually had them all breathless on the last climb atop a tree-covered hillock.

Looking down some thirty feet below, they finally saw their destination. It was a camp erected in a big circle on the cleared ground under the forest canopy and expertly hidden from spotter aircraft. There were other local recruits on the ground receiving instructional training in groups from two foreign-looking instructors. Many were wearing green headbands and wielding guns. They looked a menacing lot.

Sungkiah, after she met with Nasri, joined her fellow pahlawans for their planned trip to Pulau Sebatik. Arriving at the Batu Batu jetty in Tawau town, they could clearly sight the island ahead of them some 10 kilometres away.

"The front and eastern part of the island belongs to Malaysia; on the extreme west is Sungai Nyamuk town, which is in the Indonesian part of the island. There are no hotels or food courts on our side, but aplenty in Sungai Nyamuk. You need a border pass to get there," said the captain of their hired speedboat.

His Malay had a strong Bugis accent, prompting Dhanyal to ask, "Do the Bugis comprise the majority of the population here?"

"Yeah, they do, but we also have large numbers of the Bajau, Suluk, and Tidung. Most of them are fishermen who do their fishing on the artificial ceramic reefs that were recently constructed on the seabed off the island."

"That's interesting. But is fishing the only activity?"

"Far from it. There are a few small-holdings of oil palm and rubber, and people work there as labourers. But, if you ask me, the biggest and most rewarding activity on the island is smuggling," replied the captain, smiling away.

"I have heard of that. But tell me, is the land border on the island unfenced and people cross it at will?" asked Sungkiah.

"Yeah, you're right. It's unfenced. Illegal crossings on both sides are a daily occurrence. Lately, our police have set up an observation point to catch those engaged in human trafficking and smuggling goods across the border. Not an easy thing to do, though, as the unfenced border is almost 40 kilometres long." Then, looking towards Sungkiah, he added, "Maybe I can drop you all off at the estuary end of the river. The Indonesian village of Kampung Haji Kuning is just about three kilometres distant from there. You will find motorcycle taxis that will take you to the village, if you don't wish to walk the distance."

"I see, but we prefer to walk. How long does it take you to get us there, and can you also fetch us back, say, in about three hours?"

"Our boat ride will take about 15 minutes. No problem to fetch you back later."

The pahlawans, upon landing, made a beeline to Kampung Haji Kuning. They took the path routinely taken by the motorcycle taxis, but became acutely aware of the existence of a multitude of cross-border meandering paths (*jalan tikus*) that could also be availed of to evade police detection. They encountered no border patrols en route.

Talking to inhabitants at the village, they learnt that it had long been a preferred destination for Bugis migrants from South-Sulawesi seeking to enter Sabah illegally.

Even to the present day,the migrants ply their traditional route through Tunon Taka port in Nunukan, a regency in the Indonesian province of North Kalimantan on the Indonesia-Malaysia border. Arriving there they move west to a small jetty, where they take speedboats at a cost of less than IDR 50,000 to Bambangan on adjacent Sebatik Island. A half-hour car ride from Bambangan brings them close to Kampung Haji Kuning, from where they would illicitly cross over to Malaysia along clandestine routes.

The pahlawans also learnt that, more often than not, the migrants are aided in their illegal entry by family members or informal migration brokers who charge them a smuggling fee that also includes bribes for security officials they might encounter.

Wading into jungle areas some kilometres away from the village to get a feel of the surroundings, the pahlawans came to realise that the land boundary was just a fathomless, unguarded frontier that would long continue to haunt SCSC. The trip, however, convinced them that it was very unlikely the island could witness land intrusion from Suluk militants fleeing into Sabah from the Philippines; but the possibility could not be discounted that the multitude of clandestine channels across the border would provide ample opportunities for smuggling weapons into the state and for establishing with ease cross-border terror cells. The question was whether Bangsamoro and other ISIS-inspired pro-Islamic State militant groups had already used this security loophole to execute their plans, with recruits drawn from illegal immigrants wishing to escape from the clutches of the law.

Returning to their hotel in Tawau, Sungkiah duly noted from her mobile phone that Nasri's village lads were located in Hills Park. Turning to her two teammates, she asked, "What are the chances these lads could be bound for Pulau Sebatik next for indoctrination and advanced training in a terror cell hideout?"

"It wouldn't surprise me in the least. But wherever they might next be, I wouldn't know how Nasri would react if he became aware that they were being trained as terrorists. He would expect us to sabotage that intent," replied Dhanyal.

"I know. We'll have to wait and see," replied Sungkiah as they all walked towards the hotel café to grab some eats. There was a music band belting out some old favourites, mostly Western. An elderly couple were the only ones on the small dance floor. The pahlawans found a corner table, and Azlan soon found himself singing softly along with others in the café when the crooner came out with an evergreen Elvis Presley number.

"You have a good voice," complimented Sungkiah.

"Do you also sing? I know many Kadazans who do."

"A little, compared to the rest of my family."

"You have a big family?"

"I have five siblings and am the youngest."

"That's amazing, I'm too the youngest of five siblings. The eldest is a brother who has his own music band in Seremban. Our kampung is in Kuala Pilah."

"How about yourself?" asked Sungkiah, turning to Dhanyal, who was in age the youngest member among the pahlawans, He had stood out in training at Terendak with his physical prowess and uncanny jungle tracking skills.

"I'm from Kluang in Johor. I have only a married sister, and both my parents died in a car accident some five years ago. I'm married and have a two-year-old child."

"Sorry to hear about your parents. Does your wife know you are here on a mission with us?" asked Sungkiah.

"Certainly not. She is staying with her parents," replied Dhanyal, tucking into the chicken chop dish that he had ordered. 'I presume both of you are still single?'

"Yes," came their reply, almost in unison.

"Looks like we share the same taste buds," said Azlan when the waiter who had appeared just then placed the piquant curry mee dish they had both independently ordered in front of them. They looked at each other and smiled.

Dhanyal took his leave soon thereafter, not staying back for the dessert. The waitress that came around with the dessert order was an elderly woman with a bubbly face.

"You newlyweds?" she asked. They shook their heads, trying to stay suspended by humour.

"Well, you make a lovely couple. Will have pretty kids, for sure," she declared, before moving away with a lascivious grin. Sungkiah blushed, but Azlan reached out to hold her hand.

"Don't worry, she didn't mean to embarrass us," said Azlan in a soft voice. Just then, the band struck up the Sumazau song, and Azlan, still holding Sungkiah's hand, led her to the dance floor. The Sumazau is a popular traditional folk dance of the Kadazan Dusun, inspired by the flying patterns of eagles witnessed by farmers resting in the fields during the harvest season. It was a dance that was very familiar to Sungkiah and her performance on the floor earned her the applause of many in the café.

Returning to their table, they exchanged more intimate details of their lives thus far in their respective forces, the escapades they have had, and the roles that had been thrust on them by destiny in their current mission. It was close to midnight when they finally parted company to return to their rooms. They both realised they had shared a magical moment, one that would linger in their minds to draw them closer with the passage of time.

CHAPTER 13

*T*he Bosnian, Imran, stepped out of Saadam's estate residence wearing a pleased look. This was his third visit in many months and the ISIS leader had taken to him well, commenting on the quality of the weapons and IED material that Imran had earlier supplied. He looked at the new list of requisitions and the advance payment that he had received from the wily jihadist. He realised that things were on the move with recruitment. The specifications on the weapons and their numbers attested to that. Reaching for his phone, he called Anton to communicate the overseas order.

Anton took down the order with subdued salutations that didn't go unnoticed by Imran. "Is anything the matter?" he demanded to know at once.

"No, nothing like that. I've had two shipments on hold because of a general police raid at a fishing village longhouse I occasionally use. I have diverted their delivery to be made elsewhere. As soon as I have received them, I shall revert to you. Perhaps some of your new requirements items can be met from these consignments once they are to hand."

"Oh, OK. Let me know how things develop," answered an appeased Imran.

Anton knew that Imran was a dangerous man, one who would not hesitate to even sell his mother to get things his way. He had to tread carefully. He decided not to inform Zain on his long-time business contact, just yet.

The closing of the Pesta Kaamatan went by without a fizzle. The possibility of IED bombings that Zain had forewarned about did not take place in any townships over the entire opening week of the festival, giving the police and security personnel throughout the state much respite. Zain, however, trusted his sixth sense. To him it was only a case of delayed action on the part of pro-Islamic State militants, for the festival usually runs through the whole month, not just for the first week in May as gazetted. Things could still happen. And he was right.

Near simultaneous bomb blasts were staged by the militants in the evening on the last day of May at strategic points in Kota Kinabalu, Sandakan, and Tawau, sending the security police in these places scrambling. The IEDs were all vehicle-borne.

The blast in Sandakan was near MidTown Plaza in the city's business hub. Witnessing the event, unknown to the militants, Zain, and the police, were the two CIA agents who were at the plaza entrance. The blasts came from a car parked across the road some 50 yards from the plaza. Its roof was blown to smithereens. Fire engulfed it. Soon there was another explosion from the vehicle's fuel tank. There were screams all round. Dead and dismembered bodies were strewn on the ground near the car; elsewhere on the road, many lay injured and bleeding. It was a gruesome sight. The CIA agents rushed to help.

Police and ambulance soon descended on the scene. Arshad, who was in plainclothes, went towards the charred car as much as the flames and heat allowed. He then turned, and his eyes immediately met the Americans who were tending to some of the injured. He walked across to them.

"Did you witness the blast? Was that car there all the time?"

"We were at the entrance to the plaza when we heard the first bomb blast, followed by the burst of the car's gas tank. The car couldn't have been driven through the crowd. We think it was already parked there with a bomb inside it that was activated from outside," came the response from one of them.

"Hmm, I see. Thank you. Here's my card. Call me at this number if you recall anything else. We will be cordoning off this area soon and may impose a curfew. You'd better get a move-on."

The CIA agents quickly realised that they had been approached by a police official. They needed no further prompting to move away. Arshad saw them quickly leave.

His eyes lingered on them for a moment, for American tourists were a rare sight in Sabah.

.

Zain received the news of the blasts almost simultaneously from Arshad in Sandakan and Sungkiah in Tawau. The blast in Tawau was also near a plaza – the Eastern Plaza. It claimed a few lives, besides severely injuring dozens more. Zain knew that the moment for action for the pahlawans was drawing near; the morrow would complete their three months' stay in Sabah. He felt they had to now act tangibly on all information they had thus far gathered. His thoughts immediately flew to his old adversary, Mario. He sensed that the man was still holed up somewhere in Sandakan. He recalled Sungkiah back from Tawau to Ghosthouse for a strategic meeting of all groups. He was planning for a simultaneous raid on the premises of a dozen Chinese-run engineering and construction firms that he had shortlisted in and around Sandakan that had either aroused his suspicion or curiosity. It was going to be a mid-morning raid, he decided, spread over two days, with a priori authorisation from Arshad to search for smuggled and customs-evaded equipment. He also needed a warrant of arrest in his hands for Mario, and to have the opportunity to question him first before handing him over to the police. Arshad, still shocked by the blasts, acquiesced readily to his requests.

On the first day of the raids, all the groups were shown again the photograph of Mario and instructed by Zain that if the fugitive was spotted at any of the raided premises by any group, an immediate alert was to be sent to the other groups to descend on the premises and to seal the place.

"Bring Mario and the owner of the firm blindfolded to Ghosthouse so we can deal with them first before handing them over to the police," ruled Zain.

Success came to the pahlawans on the first day of the raid itself. The PP2 team, led by Kamal, entered an engineering works factory on the outskirts of Sandakan city at Bandar Kim Fung. The building had a high surrounding wall and a guard gate at the entrance. Kamal showed the two Nepali guards the police search warrant and told them not to make an alert call lest they wanted to face deportation. He showed them Mario's photograph, but their faces registered no hint of recognition.

Pointing next to one of the guards, Kamal asked him to escort them into the building. Entering it, Kamal went straight to the manager's office, while Samy and Su Eng went searching around the building and its double-storey annexe. Workers looked in awe at this intrusion, which had all the indications of a raid by the authorities. The two pahlawans found their man on the top floor of the annexe attending to a CNC machine that was in one of three large rooms. They nabbed him quickly and led him, handcuffed, to Kamal, who promptly messaged the news to PP1.

With the arrival of PP1, a thorough search of the premises was launched. A number of the workers were found to have no passports or work permits. It was clear that the annexe was purpose-built as a gun machining facility. Several manufactured guns and explosive devices were found stored in boxes in a room, along with unopened bags of fertilisers and aluminium nitrate. The annexe and the entire premises were sealed and, as per instructions received from Zain, group PP1 held back the illegals until Arshad arrived on the scene. In the meanwhile, the PP2 team took the manager and Mario, blindfolded, to Ghosthouse, together with some confiscated documents from the company's office. The documents were those bearing on recent equipment acquisitions by the company that the manager had filed in his locker.

When Zain arrived at Ghosthouse he found the two men handcuffed and bound to chairs, with their faces puffed up as a result of some beating that they had received at the hands of the pahlawans. The pahlawans had been waiting for Zain to commence the interrogation and had made arrangements for it to be videotaped.

"Why, if it isn't my friend Mario! You do look a bit different somehow!" sneered Zain, as he pulled up a chair to sit squarely facing his old foe. "You know the Federal Police have a warrant for your arrest. It was bad of you to let your mate Carlos get all the rap while you escaped. But, tsk! tsk! Here you're back again on the job. Who is behind all this, this time? I want full details of the supply chain — names and locations of every asshole involved in your clandestine activity. It will be good if you oblige willingly. As you're a wanted man, I could have you shot on sight, or let you free as a traitor to be found by your friends. I think you might prefer the option of a safe prison sentence with us rather than suffer the possible fate of decapitation at their hands. Wouldn't you?"

Sweat poured all over Mario, and terror filled his eyes. "I shall talk," he gulped. "The Bangsamoro group sent me here to assist them in their pro-Islamic State efforts."

"How so?"

"In manufacturing weapons that are needed to counter attacks on them by the authorities."

"To counter attacks on them? That's a new line! Killing is second nature to these terrorists. The sins they commit in the name of Islam can never be condoned. And you have fallen for their propaganda? By the way, does the name Saadam Elwan mean anything to you?" asked Zain.

"Yes, he has been enlisted from ISIS to help coordinate our action plans."

"*Our?* So, you have sold your soul to them?"

"Half my family are Moro people."

"I see. Have you seen or talked to Saadam? Where is he hiding?"

"No, I haven't. His hideout is a secret few people know about."

"But, surely, you have some idea?"

"I have heard he meets people seated behind a meshed screen, and then too always at night. He moves around a bit to escape detection."

"Where do you deliver the firearms you produce?"

"We don't. They come and collect. All middlemen. My boss here deals with them."

Zain gave the Chinaman a hard look. His hostile stare was interrupted by Su Eng, who passed him the man's identity card.

"Ah, so. Your name is Chong Yuen bin Abdullah. You're a Muslim convert. Tell me if I'm wrong. You have converted for no other reason than to improve your business. But you have entered into an evil business with an evil group. Like your friend here, only death awaits you unless you spill out to us all that we want to know. All your phone contacts, all those middlemen to whom you have sold your finished goods, and all those from whom you have received your bulk supplies. And how is it that you have been able to evade tax and enjoy security clearance? The full works. Do you understand? My boys will take you now to another room to continue the interrogation." Zain then motioned towards Kamal to take the man away.

At that moment, Zain heard a buzz on his phone. It was Arshad, trying to reach him. Getting up from his chair, he asked Samy and the others to continue the interrogation of Mario. "Make sure the phones of his Bangsamoro contacts in the Philippines are also tapped," said Zain in Malay as he went out to call Arshad.

"Hello; hope my boys have not disappointed you," Zain quipped.

"On the contrary, I'm impressed. But I believe the two kingpins are still with you?"

"Not to worry," interrupted Zain. "Once we are through with them, we will bring them over to your custody. We are trying to tap the phones of their key contacts, locally and overseas, by getting them to make the calls, and we only have a small window of time to accomplish that. Try and keep the news of the raid away from the press for a day or two, if you can. Also from police circles, as I have got the names of a few insiders in your force that will surprise you."

"What!" was Arshad's sharp reply, but Zain had already put the phone down. He wanted his men to squeeze Mario and Chong dry of all salient information on the grand design of the militants in Sabah before handing them over.

Piecing together the information they had extracted from the two hostages, and especially Mario, Zain and his pahlawans were aghast to learn that what was being hatched by the adversaries was utter mayhem on the island of Borneo, with parts of Kalimantan and Sarawak included, for the sweeping advancement of the Islamic State.

Before handing them both over to the police the next evening, Zain had coaxed Arshad over the phone to open up the factory premises for a couple of nights in the same week to allow the middlemen to gather their consignment of weapons. This would provide the opportunity for both the pahlawans and the police to trail them.

The Philippine police authorities were promptly notified about the clandestine exporters of guns and gun parts in their country, and word soon reached Arshad that they had all been caught. The double agents identified in Arshad's force were immediately arrested for their corrupt acts, which bordered on treason.

What awaited action was the alarmist information that Zain and his men had extracted from Mario, and the stream of telephone messages that they were still eavesdropping upon. The messages had to be contextually analysed. Zain was reminded of a Samurai saying, *"If you sit by the river long enough, you will see the body of your enemy float by."* He knew he had to be patient.

He had to wait for a couple of weeks before the wireless GPS trackers hidden in the boxes of firearms carried off from Mario's clandestine gun factory could be traced to a fixed location.

Zain spent a sleepless night pondering on the next course of action. He recalled that he was yet to act on the revelations of money laundering activities of some tycoons and local politicians that the Tawau timber merchant, Teh Soon Hock, had provided him. The subsequent emergence of Anton and Chong on the scene, and the realisation that a portion of the laundered money was being channelled to sustain the insurgency, worried him no ends. At the break of dawn, he made a call to Datuk Azhari.

"Good morning, Datuk. I have good news. We have caught our fugitive, Mario, here in Sandakan. He was working with the Islamic State militants through his links with the Bangsamoro. Have handed him over to the local police. The reason for this call, however, Datuk, is to seek your assistance in arranging for two senior officers from Bank Negara to come to Sandakan and examine the accounts in a bank here of a few people, and also check on the number of non-resident accounts the bank holds. There is much evidence that religious terrorists here in Sabah and Mindanao are being financed by money laundering activities, and I suspect this bank is not clean on the matter. The sooner the officers come to check on this, the better."

"I'll see what I can do. *Syabas* (Well done) on catching Mario. Don't let up on Saadam, though. He has to be captured at all costs before he creates his jihadist army."

"Of course, sir," replied Zain who promptly slumped back onto his bed.

Zain must have slept for several hours. He didn't #know the pahlawans had organised a birthday party for him quietly in the hall. He woke up with a start when they all descended on his bed with a tray containing the birthday cake, and belting out the 'Happy Birthday' song. That done, they all left for a buffet lunch at Four Points by Sheraton, where they had reserved a long table.

The place was packed with foreign tourists, but there were also many locals grouped around and enjoying their association with some high officials. That they would attract attention from others was lost on them. Indeed, the two CIA agents sitting by themselves at the food court sized them up immediately as undercover agents. Discreetly, one of them was about to use his phone to snap their group picture, when at that very moment Zain got up from his seat to fetch his dessert. His roving eyes met the man and his partner. Zain held his gaze, for their hardened faces didn't fit the image of ordinary tourists. Was it a case of one spy sensing the presence of another?

With that lingering thought in his mind, he walked over to them.

"Have we met before?" asked Zain.

"Don't think so. I'm Jim, and this is Jack," replied the man who was still holding the phone.

Zain then dropped a bombshell. "CIA agents, I presume?" he asked.

Their dropped jaws gave Zain his confirmation. "So, you're after the man too?"

Intrigued, the agents stood up to shake Zain's hand. "Please, sit down. Looks like we share the same mission," said Jack.

"Best you join us at our table. I shall be there shortly with my dessert," replied Zain.

The CIA agents waited till Zain returned to his table before joining him. Soon they were all engrossed in conversation after confirmatory exchange of their credentials.

"Intelligence gathering is what we are here for. Besides scouting around to get the feel of this place, we examine high-resolution pictures we receive continually from our satellites for any evidence of terrorist hideouts, troop movements, drug trafficking movements, and the like," observed Jim.

"That's cool. I'm sure we can work together discreetly. We're presently tracking movements of weapons and people being recruited by the militants. Also of illegal crossings into the state. It's only a question of time before we track down our main adversary. His base presently appears to be in Sandakan. We have the authority to stage surgical strikes at terror cells once we are sure of the target sites. Your satellite imagery could come in handy to us," noted Zain.

"Let us know how we can be of help. We can work out a mutually acceptable modus operandi. But the present surroundings are not conducive to a discussion on this, you agree?"

"Yes, indeed. Let us exchange our contact numbers. We can meet up elsewhere in a day or two," responded Zain.

The agents then took their leave to return to their table. Later that night, Zain announced to the pahlawans that on the morrow they would all go on a boat cruise on the Kinabatangan River. "Sooner than later we may have to prowl its banks in search of insurgents. Let's get acquainted with this mighty river. We will drive up straight to the Nature Lodge at Sepilok where we will join other tourists and behave like them. Let's plan to arrive there by 10.00 am." There was a surge of excitement, and the faces of the pahlawans uniformly lit up at the announcement which had come out of the blue.

CHAPTER 14

Zain and his pahlawans arrived at the Sepilok Nature Lodge sharply at 10.00 am but had to wait for almost an hour before they boarded with the other tourists the minibusses that took them to the Kinabatangan Nature Lodge. This was the starting point for the river cruise; its location was on the banks of the Kinabatangan River in the Kinabatangan Wildlife Sanctuary. The approximately two-and-a-half-hour bus ride from Sepilok took them past oil palm plantations, small townships, and villages of "orang sungai" (river people) to Kampung Bilit, where the buses halted.

"This is a small village populated by fisherfolk who also do some rice and orchard planting. They are of mixed ancestry, including Tambanua, Idahan, Dusun, Suluk, Bugis, Bajaus, and Chinese, but all of them speak Malay. Their fishing activity is not just confined to the river, but extends also to the Tanjung Bulat Oxbow Lake. This lake is one of many that inundate the lower Kinabatangan flood plain," said the driver of the minibus that Zain and his mates had boarded.The lines were spoken in well-rehearsed, unfaltering English, which did not go unnoticed by the pahlawans.

"Is it a big lake?" Su Eng wanted to know.

"Yes, it is huge, covering an area of about 95 hectares, with depths up to 30 metres. Importantly, it is free of crocodiles. This favours outdoor activities on the lake. A small tributary of it connects to the Kinabatangan River."

A short boat ride across the Kinabatangan River took Zain and his pahlawans, along with the others, to the Kinabatangan Nature Lodge. They relaxed at the restaurant in the lodge until 3.30 p.m. before donning their lifejackets and boarding the boats for the scheduled two-hour river cruise. The boats were of varying sizes, but Zain and his pahlawans managed to pack themselves into one. Their tour guide appeared to be an old hand at his job. His name was Hairol. Wielding his binoculars, he wasted no time in extolling the unique ecosystem that was around them.

"Much of this lower Kinabatangan River area has been gazetted under the Kinabatangan Wildlife Sanctuary. No logging is permitted in these parts. By the way, does anyone here know why this place is called Kinabatangan?" asked the guide, half-turning around.

Everyone registered a stupefied look on their faces. The guide fell silent for a while, as though he was in no particular hurry to disclose the answer. It seemed as if he was holding back some highly prized secret.

Finally, after what seemed an eternity, Hairol turned to face them with a wry smile on his lips. "The name Kinabatangan is derived from *Kina* (China) and *Batang* (large river). This reflects the trade links that existed between China and Borneo as far back as 631 AD."

There were quizzical looks all around. Zain and his party needed no invitation to google the word *batang*. They were surprised to learn that the word has been used in the past to mean a tributary. All the same, the explanation of the name sounded farfetched to Zain, who refrained from offering a comment.

After a while, Hairol resumed his chat. "There are six different species of primates living here in this rainforest. Let's hope we can at least spot some of them on this trip."

An air of expectancy gripped everyone, all wanting to catch their first glimpse of anything wild at all. They were not disappointed. As the boat turned a corner on the meandering river, the guide struck an exultant note.

"There, there, look on the starboard side. Wow, aren't you people lucky! Can you see the big fellow – the orangutan – sprawled on the top branch? He is staring at us. And, oh, another is joining him!" Hairol pointed his hand excitedly at the treetops to let the others following him know of his find, while Zain focussed his video-camera sunglasses on the primates. He was himself amazed at the technology resting on his nose.

As the boat moved further upstream, the stillness of the jungle was palpable, broken only by the screeching of flying birds of various hues of colour, the sounds of howler monkeys, and the occasional distinct mating calls of gibbons that were out of sight. Surprisingly, there were no

173

mosquitoes to bother them. They could detect no movement on the banks for a while until a group of long-nosed, pot-bellied proboscis monkeys who were camouflaged in the trees suddenly dropped to the water's edge. Their diving and frolicking stunts in the water were a delight to watch. All the boats immediately slowed down and, with their engines switched off, floated toward the banks. The tourists could now also clearly see more monkeys in the trees boisterously cavorting about, leaping daringly from tree to tree. The clicking cameras did not appear to bother them one bit.

"What do they feed on?" enquired Su Eng of the guide.

"They are seasonal eaters. They eat mostly fruit from January to May, and mostly leaves from June to December. Other monkeys enjoy the odd snack of a bird or a lizard, but not these guys. They are pure vegetarians!" replied the guide, displaying a sense of humour.

As the boats pressed on deeper into the jungle, ample sights of birds came into view, including the Oriental pied hornbills as they flew over the river to rest on the forest trees. The guide reeled off a few names of other avians that were perched on the overhanging branches of the trees, many of whom were migratory birds. They then saw him furtively scanning the treetops at both banks with his binoculars, as if in search of something. Moments later, a cry of delight escaped his lips as he finally spotted through a clearing in the trees what he was searching for — a pair of majestic Rhinoceros hornbills. The value of a good guide was clear to Zain and his mates. Hairol's trained eyes were able to spot camouflaged wildlife that would have otherwise escaped the notice of others.

The canopy of the jungle on this stretch was simply seething with birdlife. There were also egrets of various types, just content on walking in the water at the edge of the banks. Dhanyal exchanged seats with one of his mates, as he wanted to take a video of the scene. Suddenly there was a commotion at the water's edge among the egrets, as one of them fell prey to a lurking crocodile. The rest of the flock quickly took to the air, and unbelievably, the whole colony of birds in the trees fluttered off the branches and burst into a cacophony of angry sounds to register their protest at this intrusion. Everyone was spellbound watching this wildlife scene – a bonus for the trip granted by Mother Nature. Dhanyal couldn't believe his luck as well. He registered it with a smile that stretched from ear to ear.

A further hour into the ride, Hairol again helped the pahlawans spot a couple of long-tailed Macaque monkeys feasting on a crab. The guide's mispronunciation of the name elicited muffled laughter from Zain and those seated next to him. But the guide quickly regained their attention when he went on to narrate that Macaque monkeys have found preferred use in animal testing in the field of neuroscience, but being carriers of several viruses, they are dangerously unsuitable as pets. He added that some studies have even attested to their involvement in the species-to-species jump of many retroviruses to humans. He stopped as the sound of an approaching speedboat reached him and all others. It was travelling at a high speed, causing their boat to rock badly by the sudden rush of pushed-up water towards it. Zain who was still wearing his video camera sunglasses immediately spotted Anton among them. He wondered what Anton's agenda was this time.

"I suspect the son of a bitch is playing a double game. He needs to be snuffed out," said Samy who had also spotted him.

Zain remained silent. His mind was weighing the possibility of there being a terror cell deep in the forest with unhindered riverine access to guns and ammunition.

It was Kamal who broke into his thoughts with a query to the guide.

"Any hope of seeing a pygmy elephant or rhinoceros?"

"We have not been able to spot a rhinoceros yet on this stretch, but sighting pygmy elephants should not be a problem a bit further on," came his reply.

Soon, a mist started forming ahead of them, darkening the jungle and giving it an even more ominous look. Almost simultaneously a symphony of eerie jungle sounds began to fill the misty air. Zain's thoughts flew back to his boat ride adventure the previous year on Temenggor Lake while stalking clandestine gunsmiths holed up in the ancient Belum Rainforest. He wondered whether his new mission might give rise to a similar situation in the Kinabatangan jungle.

Kinabatangan Wildlife

Clockwise from top to bottom:

Borneo pygmy elephants (*Photo credit: Denis Luyten,Public domain, via Wikimedia Commons*);

Proboscis monkey (*Photo credit: Charles J. Sharp, CC BY-SA 4.0, via Wikimedia Commons*);

Blue-headed Pitta bird (*Photo credit: Weng Keong Liew (liewwk) @ Oriental Bird Club; reproduced with permission*);

Lar gibbon (*Photo credit: Wikimedia Commons, JJ Harrison, license CC-BY-SA 3.0*)

He was brought back from his reverie by an excited shout from Dhanyal.

"There, look behind us on the left bank; I spotted a grey creature moving about!"

The boat immediately slowed and turned an angle. The boats behind similarly manoeuvred towards the port side.

Hairol focussed his binoculars on the movement. "Yes, indeed, they are pygmy elephants. There are three of them, just coming out. We shall turn the boat around to get closer. Don't want to frighten them off."

A few moments later, all the boats turned in unison to return to the lodge, as the 2-hour duration for the cruise was already up.

Arriving back at the lodge, they profusely thanked Hairol for the enjoyable ride. Zain requested his call card and noted that he was an ex-Sarawak Ranger, now settled in Sukau.

The seafood dinner that was served at the restaurant was delicious. This was followed by a brief presentation to all the tourists on the wildlife in the Kinabatangan area, and also the conservation programme undertaken by Nature Lodge Kinabatangan. Some of the tourists responded to the request to make voluntary contributions to the wildlife fund. At 8.00 p.m., the tourists not staying overnight at the lodge prepared themselves for the return journey. It was close to 10.00 p.m. when Zain and his mates arrived back at their Villa Permai guesthouse, pleased to have had the whole day together for bonding. Whatever qualm Zain might have had for sneaking in the pleasure trip while on assignment went out the window the moment he spotted Anton, as this confirmed his fears that irregular patrolling of major riverine routes by SCSC had worked into the hands of militants to establish their clandestine cells with unhindered access to firearms.

....

CHAPTER 15

*T*he Bank Negara officials arrived in Sandakan within three days of Zain's request. Their search at the bank revealed a plethora of non-compliant discrepancies that shocked them. Working discreetly with the bank manager, they identified two insiders in the bank's employ responsible for the misdeeds and cover-up. Zain was made privy to information on clients of the bank who were in his list of suspects for clandestine activities, including the names that the Tawau timber merchant, Teh Soon Hock, had provided him, as well as on the accounts held by Anton, Imran, and Chong.

By way of a bonus, they also provided him the names of two companies, both based in Tawau, that had raised red flags in respect to their transactions through this bank for local property investment and foreign money transfers.

The corrupt insiders at the bank were immediately suspended and placed under police custody for embezzlement and other pending charges. Zain promptly sent Kamal and his team in search of Imran. They were also asked to track on their mobile phones the movements of the middlemen who had come to secure weapons from the factory. Sungkiah and her team were directed to check up on the activities of the two miscreant organisations in Tawau, and while there, to also look into the whereabouts of Nasri's village lads.

On his part, Zain sought a meeting with the CIA duo. He was sure they had more information on Saadam than they were prepared to divulge. They agreed to meet up with him for dinner at 7th Heaven, an American restaurant, the following day.

Samy decided he would meet up with Anton as a prelude to the hunt for Imran. He wanted to test Anton's promised loyalty as an ally. Without mentioning his eavesdropped pickup of Imran's name from Anton's phone, Samy asked Anton to list all the names of his clients whose orders for firearms he had entertained. Anton obliged, but missed out Imran's name on the paper that Samy had given him.

"Are you sure you have not omitted anyone?"

"Sure, sir," responded Anton.

Samy pulled out his revolver and in a flash, thrust the barrel into Anton's mouth.

"We told you what your fate would be if you double-cross us," said Samy with a stern face and voice.

Anton went white, trembling with fear. Samy withdrew the gun and gave him back the list. The name "Imran, Bosnian," was quickly scribbled on it.

"That's better. Now find out where he is and arrange to meet up with him. One of my men will act like your assistant when you go to meet him. Be natural, and don't give him any cause for suspicion. If you do, both you and Imran will be killed the very next instant. Is that understood?"

Anton nodded and did as he was told, and the meeting was fixed for the next morning at a local café.

Entering the café early, Kamal went up to take a seat by Anton's side and to pose as his aide, while Samy and Su Eng occupied a nearby table. All awaited the arrival of Imran. They saw a car pull up at the entrance and two men alighted, one of them a policeman. Both looked around the place and then made a direct line towards Anton, who got up from his chair to greet Imran. Introductions over, Anton leaned towards Imran.

"I have a consignment that has not been taken up. Here's the list. The pistols are not exactly the make that you wanted; they are a higher-end Glock – Glock 18C, and therefore, a bit more costly. The price differential is USD 30. The Ruger 9 mm carbine is also what I have in stock. It will accept a Glock magazine. If you can make your pick, I can arrange to have them delivered to you."

Imran studied the list and the pamphlet that Anton had given him. He suddenly became apprehensive. It was normal to have the replacement firearms sighted before any commitment to purchase transpires. And Anton had not shown him any specimen samples. He whispered something to the policeman who was seated beside him, who abruptly got up and moved behind Kamal, demanding to see his identity card.

In a flash, Samy and Su Eng, with pistols in hand, sprang into action. They handcuffed both Imran and the policeman, bundled them into their car blindfolded, and sped away to Ghosthouse.

The Bosnian proved a tough nut to crack, despite the beating he received from Samy and Kamal. Soon Zain arrived on the scene. He asked for Imran's phone. He scanned the list of contacts and found Anton's name. Saadam's name was not there. Next, he went through the photos and was surprised that over 4,000 images were stored in the album. Going through some recent additions, he suddenly stopped. There was a clear picture taken of a madrasah in which someone in overflowing Arab clothing was receiving a gift of copies of the Holy Koran from a donor. Zain's adrenaline soared at the sight. He thrust the photograph in front of the Bosnian.

"Is this Saadam – the man to whom you are supplying the guns?" asked Zain.

"I don't know who he is," came the swift reply.

"Then why did you take the picture?"

"I was invited there."

Zain gave him a hard look. The Bosnian was lying through his teeth. Taking out his pistol, Zain shot him on his leg. The man fell from his chair, bleeding and groaning in pain. But he still refused to acknowledge knowing Saadam. Then Zain did the unthinkable. He ordered a videotaping to be set up, and abruptly left the room. He returned, donning a head cover and a facial mask. Taking a sword in his hand, he moved towards the Bosnian. He made him kneel and face the camera, and then standing over him, brought the blade of the sword towards his throat. He was enacting the ISIS mode of beheading. The pahlawans were suddenly witnessing a vengeful side of Zain, an inner demon, they had not associated with his normal character.

In a miasma of sweat and fear, Imran screamed for mercy. Zain was unwavering. "You have just the one chance to trade your life for the information that we seek. Tell us where Saadam is hiding."

"In an oil palm estate….." quavered Imran before he fainted.

The pahlawans scrambled to note all nearby palm oil estates and small holdings they could access through their mobiles, but the Bosnian recovered soon enough to identify the estate.

"It's less than 20 kilometres from here," announced Kamal, studying his Google map.

"OK, before we raid Saadam's hideout, let us weed out more information from this son of a bitch," remarked Samy, who was bandaging his shot leg.

"He oversees a madrassah in the estate, and recruits people to the cause," confessed Imran.

"Where does he conduct the indoctrination and militant training?" asked Zain.

"In camps, I do not know."

"How do you contact him?"

"I don't, except by going to the madrasah in the estate and sending word to him through someone there. His bodyguard will then come and fetch me."

"OK, draw us the route that leads to his hideout from the estate entrance," said Zain, handing him a piece of paper and a pen.

With the sketch of the route in his hands, Zain asked SuEng to guard the hostages while he and the others rode out to Saadam's hideout.

The raid was swift, but the house was empty of inhabitants. From the neighbouring house, Haji Jalah poked his head out, wondering about the intruders. Kamal sighted him and immediately dragged him out to question him on the whereabouts of his infamous neighbour. His denial of any knowledge about his neighbour irked the pahlawans, who ruffled him up to learn finally that Saadam had set up the madrasah in the estate in which he had been roped in to help, and that the man was in the habit of taking regular outstation trips.

"Where has he gone? And when is he due back?" asked Zain.

"Don't know, tuan. He always returns after two weeks," replied Haji Jalah.

"In that case, you're coming with us for the same period," said Zain, pushing the man over to Samy

The pahlawans then planted their spy gadgets and left the place.

Back at Ghosthouse, Zain pumped Jalah again to disclose where Saadam had gone. "Surely, you have some hint of that. You must have seen the people who came to fetch him."

"Some people came to fetch him in a jeep. Some days back. Never seen them before," stammered Jalah, somewhat unconvincingly. The answer was greeted by a punch on his face. He instantly bled at the mouth.

"I remember one of them coming to the madrasah before," spat out Jalah almost instantly.

Zain then contacted Arshad and told him about their encounter with three people who had dealings with Saadam.

"We need you to hold them in your custody without bail so as not to alert Saadam. The offence is abetting terrorism."

"If you say so," replied Arshad good-humouredly.

Pleased as punch about his arrangements with the police, Zain sat down with his pahlawans to figure out where Saadam could have headed. Could his destination be the same as where Mario's guns had reached?

Zain's unspoken query was answered by Kamal. "The two groups of middlemen who came to fetch the cargo of guns headed in two directions, the nearest being to the Kabili-Sepilok Forest Reserve, and the farthest to Pekan Beluran, where we have previously been. Remember that village dominated by the Suluks? The signals from our GPS wireless tracking device placed in the cargo boxes have indicated this. The taps that we placed on the phones of the middlemen have corroborated this, particularly in the case of Pekan Beluran; but the cargo to the forest reserve changed hands at Kampung Bambangan. I'm hypothesizing it must have gone to its destination from there by riverine transport for a section of the journey and then overland along a nature trail."

He paused to continue. "If you ask me, if I were him, I would pick a remote area deep within the Kabili-Sepilok Forest Reserve to be my training camp. According to the Google map, such an area can be found in the south and east of the Sepilok Orangutan Rehabilitation Centre."

"Bingo! Exactly what I think," exulted Samy.

"If only we had Saadam's phone number to track the man, whether he is in any of these two places," lamented Kamal.

"We have a contact at Pekan Beluran. Jamil is his name. I remember attending to him. We can contact him for news there," chipped in Su Eng.

"Yes, of course. What about the forest reserve? How sure are we he has gone there?" Kamal pressed.

"Wait a minute! Perhaps we can seek the assistance here of our American friends," said Zain. "We can ask them if they can spot any unusual activity in the forest area in their satellite imagery that can guide us. I'm meeting them for dinner tonight."

"I'm wondering what the two can accomplish by themselves," enquired Su Eng.

"What they are doing is some satellite reconnaissance work and trying to relate that to bits and pieces of information they pick up on the ground, to get some concrete evidence of clandestine activities, such as militant groupings, drug trafficking, and the like. The CIA will then assess the information and pass it on to Malaysian security agencies at MinDef. The CIA is always known to do their work surreptitiously. It was pure luck on our part to bump into the two agents. However, I'm not going to spill out our discovery of Saadam's estate hideout to them. At least, not just yet. As far as they are concerned, we are just trailing the passage of firearms into interior regions of the state," replied Zain. The pedagogic answer silenced further comments.

Later as Zain was preparing to leave for the dinner meeting, Su Eng approached him, "Boss, can I ask you something?"

"Shoot," replied Zain.

"Would you have gone through with the act if the Bosnian had not yielded? Or was it just an act to frighten him out of his skin?"

"Hmm! I guess I'll have to ask my doppelgänger about that," replied Zain, smiling as he looked into the hallway mirror, and gave his hair a comb before setting out.

Walking towards the restaurant, Zain briefly toyed with the idea of asking SAC Arshad to join him, but then he recalled the reticence of MinDef in getting the CIA involved in the hunt for Saadam. His unexpected links with them, therefore, had to be kept under wraps for a while.

In a quiet corner of the restaurant following dinner, the CIA duo examined the zoom-in remote-sensing images received on their mobile of the Kabili-Sepilok forest area that Zain had asked them to check.

"They are taken from sensors on board our agency's secret satellite that is in a geosynchronous equatorial orbit," explained Jim.

Nodding, Zain peered over several real-time images of the virgin jungle areas to the south and east of the Sepilok Orangutan Rehabilitation Centre on the 12-inch screen magnifier that Jim had attached to his mobile phone. There was evidence of persistent light flicker in one zoom-in view of the forest area that was otherwise shrouded in darkness. The only other lighted area was much farther east, at Kampung Bambangan. Zain quickly jotted down the coordinates of the location.

"I think we might have spotted a training camp there. I shall have to request SCSC to send a drone over the area and see what more can be picked up at daylight," remarked Zain.

"Yes, certainly worth investigating," responded Jack.

Some small talk then followed, at the end of which Zain asked them in a low voice, "There's something I've been hesitating to ask you both about. It concerns Saadam. What's the man like?"

"A devil in disguise. Has no compassion whatsoever, and wants to impose his cruel brand of Islam on the world. He has sworn to kill all fakirs on sight. We nearly caught him in Syria, but the son of a gun managed to escape to Pakistan, where he was operating on the northern borders of that country until his sudden appearance here, which caught all of us by surprise," replied Jim.

"Don't worry, he won't escape my clutches. Do you have a picture of him?"

"Yes, sure," said Jim, who showed him the photograph that was on his phone. Zain copied it to his phone. "But we have received intelligence reports about his assistant, who is on his way here from Afghanistan," continued Jim.

"What?" responded a surprised Zain.

"Yes, and we suspect he is making his way here from North Kalimantan," added Jack.

"So, the Indonesian Jamaah Ansharut Daulah (JAD) terror group has also been roped in by ISIS for their mission here?" asked Zain, rather rhetorically.

"You will be surprised to know that among the foreign students and lecturers that have come to your public universities from the Middle East there are a few that have strong leanings towards radical Islam. They see your country with its predominantly Muslim population as an ideal geographical location to spread their roots here. Also, they sense that the people here are generally friendly and unsuspecting. Saadam and his assistant may turn out to be not your only cause for worry."

A few more drinks later, Zain took his leave, promising to meet them again if he received any information on Saadam from his network of local contacts.

Stepping out of the restaurant, he headed towards his parked car. For a moment, his usual alertness deserted him as he was engrossed with other thoughts rushing in his head. It was only when he was within a few feet of the car that he saw from the corner of his eye a motorbike heading fast towards him carrying a pillion rider who was wielding a pistol. The first shot caught Zain in the shoulder as he instinctively protected his head while falling to his knees. Two more bullets hit the car and a final one grazed his leg as he quickly slid to the side of the car, away from the speeding bike. The incident instantly brought back memories of the tragic shootout that he had witnessed at the road junction restaurant in Kuala Lumpur before the start of the mission. He knew that this was a close shave. If not for the proximity of the car that served as a barrier to deflect the shots, he might have been a sitting duck. The shots brought out the security stationed at the entrance of the restaurant and also the CIA agents. The latter rushed towards Zain, who was up by then.

"I'm afraid I have caught a bullet on my right shoulder. The two men on the motorbike were clearly waiting for me. Couldn't make them out, as they had their helmets on," said Zain.

The Americans took him straight to the Emergency Unit at the hospital and left before Arshad, who was alerted on the incident, arrived. Kamal and Samy, upon hearing the news dashed to the hospital. They were relieved he was not seriously injured, but couldn't help speculating on the cause. Had their cover been blown? If so, how? Were the Americans the cause? Could they have been tailed, with interceptions of their mobile phones? How could the adversaries know otherwise that Zain was meeting up with them? Could Haji Jalah be the man who blew their cover somehow from the prison? Or was it the corrupt policeman who was with Imran? Could he have recognized Zain who'd had several meetings with Arshad at the police station? The questions had no immediate answers, but they knew they all had to be on their vigil from that moment onwards.

With the bullet removed from his arm, Zain opted not to be admitted, and left with Kamal and Samy to Ghosthouse for a week or two of recuperation, as insisted upon by the doctor. But no sooner than he had arrived there, he put a call through to Brigadier General Othman for a drone survey of the forest areas at Kabili-Sepilok and Hills Park, where guerrilla training for recruits by the militants was suspected. Zain felt the burning urge as he spoke to be out there on the field and blast the terror cells into oblivion. If not for Su Eng's insistence for daily dressings on his wound, he would have found an excuse to leave the premises. She fussed over him, even preparing some meals for him with a dash of herbal elements to hasten the wound healing. Zain was touched by her loyalty and professionalism.

Her attention towards his health did not go unnoticed by Kamal and Samy. Not to be outdone, one day Samy elected to be the chef and made for them all a spicy chicken curry, which they enjoyed with the traditional Bugis dish of *burasak* (a variant of *ketupat*, a rectangular rice dumpling encased in banana leaf) that Kamal somehow managed to get for the occasion. Over this period, the trio along with Zain went over all the bits of information hacked from their eavesdropped phones to get a sense of the plans and movements of their adversaries.

Barely a week into his recuperation period, Zain was found one morning groaning with pain on his shoulder and nursing a temperature. Su Eng examining the wound on his shoulder found some evidence of infection. She turned towards Kamal and Samy who had gathered around Zain. "Look guys, I'll have to dash down to the nearest pharmacy to get some antibiotics and replensish also the stock of medication in my doctor's bag. At the moment I have given him some Paracetamol. That should settle his fever. Shall be back soon."

"Give me the list, I shall get them for you," offered Samy.

"No, Samy, I'll have to go myself. Without a medical certificate they won't dispense certain medications."

Anxiety grew in the Ghosthouse when two hours after her departure there was still no word forthcoming from Su Eng. She had not responded to a call to her cell phone from Kamal or to the audio message that Samy had additionally sent her. To their chagrin, they realised that she had taken their only car. Kamal dashed to Zain's room and found him asleep. He picked up his phone and saw the urgent message which instantly paled his face. The message read "Gone 1".

"Fuck!" spat Zain as he jumped out of bed and grabbed the phone from Kamal. The bastards have kidnapped her. The message was from her smartwatch, not her handphone. Her current location indicates she is in the Sepilok area. I have now to signal her handphone to self-destruct. No choice." His face was grim, and his voice was strangled.

"That's the forest area where they have the orangutan sanctuary. Why on earth are her kidnappers taking her there?" asked a bewildered Samy.

"Probably they have a hidden terror cell in the area and she is being taken there to treat some injured people. Or more probably as a bait to draw us all there. The self-destruction of her phone will also confirm to them that we know where they are," observed Kamal.

Zain was about to respond when his phone rang. The call was from Brigadier General Othman at the SCSC headquarters in Lahad Datu. He was not aware of Zain's injury and the attempt on his life. The general was all excited with the news he had in hand about the drone video cameras showing groups of men wearing jungle green outfits and black head covers chasing after dogs with knives in their hands. "They are practicing ISIS-style quick executions with dogs as their prey," said the general.

"How dreadful! But I have some distressing news General.One of my team members, Dr Su Eng, was kidnapped a few hours ago while she was at the pharmacy getting some medication."

"What?!!" exclaimed the general. " Any idea where they have taken her?"

"We have traced her whereabouts to Sepilok, General. Our trail of illicit guns also leads to the Kabili-Sepilok area. Probably the militants have a base camp there. Conceivably our man Saadam might also be there conducting the training. We have to locate their camp and mount a surgical strike to rescue our kidnapped member. If Saadam is there, we will not miss him either," replied Zain, who appeared more composed by then.

"Hmm," mused the general. "The area is close to the Sepilok Orang Utan Rehabilitation Centre and heavily forested. This rules out helicopter attacks or aerial bombings. Also as much as your colleague, we want to capture Saadam alive. Your suggestion of a stealth surgical strike is the only way. But I want the army involved as well."

"I agree, sir. My other team members are still in Tawau. They are not aware of the kidnapping. I shall be recalling them back to Sandakan."

"Noted. Let's meet at the Sandakan Police HQ at around 11 am tomorrow morning. I shall invite SAC Arshad and the commandant of the army camp at Kinabatangan to join us. Keep the matter under your belt for the moment," replied the general.

"Sure, General. We shall be there," replied Zain.

Just as Zain put the phone down, there was a call from Sungkiah in Tawau.

"Hello, sir. We're still shocked to hear about the shooting. Hope you're recovering well."

"Well, that's history and nothing compared to what I'm about to tell you. Su Eng was kidnapped by militants this morning while at the pharmacy. Unfortunately, she had gone there alone. We have traced her whereabouts to Sepilok. We believe the militants have a camp there. We want you all back here. A rescue is being organised within a day or two," said Zain.

"*Alamak!* (Oh, dear!) I hope I can get my hands on these devils. I will rip their guts out," replied an agitated Sungkiah.

"You will get the chance. Any news from your front?" asked Zain.

"Yes, we have confirmed that Nasri's village recruits are still at Hills Park. Surprised to learn that the fruit vendor at Kampung Attap Tengah was among the group that came to get the village recruits. I recognised him from the photograph that Nasri had sent me."

"Fancy that!" commented Zain.

Sungkiah also had news on the two organisations that were involved in money laundering. "One of them is an accounting firm and the other a commercial law firm. We found out that the law firm was instrumental in quietly helping a local politician set up an investment company dealing in real estate. The politician has recently been accused of accepting bribes from a construction company. The accounting firm, on the other hand, has many money lenders as their clients, and word has it around here that it is the firm to approach if one wants to carry out transfers in foreign countries. Surprise of surprises, Anton is one of their clients."

"That's interesting. Don't worry; the long arm of the law will soon reach them. I want you and the team back at Ghosthouse as quickly as you can," said Zain.

"OK, sir. We should be back there tonight," replied Sungkiah.

CHAPTER 16

*E*arly the following morning, Zain had a group meeting with the pahlwans to discuss Su Eng's capture and strategise on her rescue plan in concert with the impending raid on the terror cell.

"I should have put my foot down. She should not have ventured out alone. We can only hope and pray that they have not harmed her," voiced Zain shaking his head.

"The only information that she can spill about us is how many of us are out there looking for Saadam, and perhaps about our hideout here if they resort to torture her or subject her to a lie detection test," said Kamal.

"I'm sure she won't succumb that easily,' responded Samy. "But what piques me is why she was abducted. They must have been aware that she was a doctor and knew where she was holed up. A chance came their way and they took it? How did they know that she was going out alone this morning and where to? Is our place bugged?"

There was silence all around. Samy had raised valid questions.

"I share Samy's concern. We need to check this place all over again for possible bugging that might have happened at some point when we were all away. Also, more than ever, we should install a closed-circuit television surveillance system here immediately." The words came from Azlan.

"I agree," said Zain. "We shall first go through every inch of this place again to see if someone has bugged it. And Azlan, you're the best among us with electronics. I shall leave it to you to arrange for the CCTV system to be installed as immediately as possible. The system must lend for real-time viewing in our cell phones."

"That's how it shall be, sir. I shall act on it today," responded Azlan with several nods of his head.

"Assuming Su Eng is still clinging on to her watch and projecting it merely as a health monitor aid to her captors, we shall be able to fix her location in the enemy camp in real-time. But it has to be before her watch battery drains out. Samy and Sungkiah will be charged with locating and rescuing her once the raid begins. But we have to plan it carefully. We will know after the meeting with General Othman later this morning how we're going to go about it. But before that, we need to locate the pharmacy where Su Eng might have gone and where she had parked the car. I'm sure she would have picked the nearest pharmacy from here. I want all four of you - Azlan, Dhanyal, Samy and Kamal - to attend to this straight away." spoke Zain.

Getting up from his chair, Zain felt the blood draining from his face. The wound on his shoulder was continuing to hurt him. Samy noticed this and asked Sungkiah whether she had any antibiotics in her possession.

"May have a few Augmentin tablets still left. Why?"

"Give them to the boss. His wound is infected and he needs antibiotics which Su Eng was on her way to get."

"Thank you all for your concern", responded Zain. "Samy, see if you can persuade the pharmacist to part with some more of this antibiotic under Su Eng's name if she had been there. Take Azlan with you. If confirmed that she was there, I want Azlan to check their CCTV footing to see if anything unusual was playing out. Also, if you find the car, you should bring it back as soon as possible."

"When is your appointment at the Sandakan Police HQ?" asked Kamal.

"Oh, yes, around 11 am. I want you and Sungkiah to join me at the meeting," replied Zain as he reached for a glass of water to swallow the antibiotic tablet he had popped into his mouth.

Zain with his two pahlawans were punctual, arriving at the Sandakan Police HQ on the dot at 11 am. En route, he received the news that Su Eng was kidnapped as she stepped out of her car parked close to the pharmacy.

SAC Arshad greeted them upon their arrival and ushered them two floors up to the meeting room. Brigadier General Othman was already there with the army commandant.

"I have been piecing together the information that we have so far gathered from our drone surveys and from ASP Zain and his team. Saadam is no longer in the estate house where he had been hiding all this while. He has taken to the field to train militants. There is evidence from the drone survey of a terrorist camp in the Kabili-Sepilok Forest Reserve, which is less than 30 kilometres from the estate. We suspect our man could be there, and I want him captured alive. The attack on the camp has to be well planned and executed. The matter has become a bit complicated because one member of Zain's team who is also a medical doctor - Dr Su Eng - was kidnapped yesterday morning by militants. From GPS tracking we have noted her location to be also in Sepilok. She is probably being held captive in the same terrorist camp. Our attack, therefore, will have a two-fold objective: to rescue Dr Su Eng and to capture alive the ISIS infiltrator Saadam. The raid has to be swift and take the adversary by complete surprise," began Brigadier General Othman. No one disagreed.

"We need as much intelligence as we can gather about the camp and its environment before we execute the strike," commented the army commandant.

"I agree. We need to examine both aerial and ground intelligence about the camp. To be sure, they will have their spies posted at key areas of the forest reserve. And don't forget, they have dogs to alert them as well. If Saadam is indeed there in person, he might have also placed mines on the ground leading to the camp," said Zain.

Kamal then sought permission to speak.

"You all know about the illegal firearms factory on the outskirts of Sandakan that we exposed to the police.

Based on our tracking of weapons sourced from this factory, we have learnt that one consignment was headed for the Kabili-Sepilok Forest Reserve with transit at Kampung Bayangan. This means there is a terror cell deep in the forest there. The insurgents could have made their way there using one of the many nature trails that exist in the region. Their starting point could have been either the Sepilok Orangutan Rehabilitation Centre or the Sepilok Jungle Resort. Both these areas are accessible by car," said Kamal.

"Where exactly might their camp be?" asked the army commandant. "

The coordinates of the camp sighted by the drone indicate that it lies to the south and east of the Sepilok Orangutan Sanctuary, at the one end of which is where the resort is," responded the general.

"I'm wondering General whether or not we might benefit from a visit first to the forest reserve disguised as tourists. Possibly, we may be able to ascertain the best land approach to their camp. Once we bring some feedback to this table, the tactical details for the surgical strike can be worked out," opined the army commandant.

"That's a fair comment," chipped in SAC Arshad. "We can ask the police on the ground there, and also the forest rangers, to help us in the reconnaissance work, if need be "

"I think the less the others know about our mission, the better," interrupted the general. "We can perhaps settle for just one experienced and trustworthy forest ranger to be included. If you all agree with the commandant's suggestion, can we pick the team to do the scouting work?" Pausing to get general agreement, he continued. "May I suggest seven persons in total, three each from ASP Zain's team and the army, and the forest ranger that will be identified to us by SAC Arshad. Zain can lead the group."

There was no dissent to the general's suggestion and his further suggestion that the trip to the forest reserve be made three days hence, on a Sunday, when they all can quietly blend in with the tourists.

"We shall meet again on Monday afternoon following the forest reserve scouting trip to decide on the plan of attack," remarked the general, wearing a satisfied look on his face at the prospect of capturing Saadam.

CHAPTER 17

Zain preoccupied himself over the next couple of days with examining the various Google satellite pictures of the area ahead of the trip. He was tossing in his mind what might be the best stealth approach to the camp. The idea soon began to crystallize in his head that the upper reaches of the Kabili River would afford them all the cover they would need to launch the stealth attack day or night, and also to get back safely by the river route.

Kamal, after several failed attempts, finally managed to contact Jamil, who was happy to narrate events in his village.

"Some weeks back, a group of Bangsamoro fighters from the Turtle Islands came to our village. They hid here a week, and after collecting some cargo, went northwards. I came to know that they were heading for Golong," said Jamil.

Kamal, studying the map of the area, wondered about their choice of Golong. It struck him, looking at the Google satellite map, that there was thick jungle extending north and west of the place, ideal for establishing a terror cell. The proximity of Golong to Pulau Jambongan also hinted that those insurgents landing on the island might form the bulk of the manpower for the terror cell. He communicated his thoughts to Zain who concurred with him and called in the rest of the pahlawans to hear Kamal out. They all agreed that the entire stretch from Pulau Jambongan to the hinterland of Golong had to be subject to drone surveillance.

"One more area that needs to be included is Pulau Sebatik, especially the area just beyond our international border. This is where I suspect they will finally build their mother of all terror cells that will hit Tawau and neighbouring areas," voiced Samy.

"I suppose that with cells established at Sandakan, Beluran, and Sebatik, they think they will give SCSC a run for their money," remarked Sungkiah.

"That's fanciful thinking. But there is no denying that theirs will be a jihadist effort all the same, which we cannot take lightly. We have little choice but to destroy these cells in their nascent stage. God willing, we will," observed Zain.

Retiring to his room, Zain went into a retrospective mood and remained so for much of the next day. It had been months since he and his team were in Sabah. He missed his family. Acting on impulse, he called Mariam. They talked for quite a while until his daughter Zaleha came on the line, snatching the phone off her mother. Zain didn't realize she had turned into a chatterbox. Her utterances were sweet words to his ears; he didn't expect pearls of wisdom from his impish daughter telling him to be careful when he goes out to capture bad people and to avoid eating unhealthy food.

He was not happy telling Mariam a white lie about him needing to go to East Malaysia on and off to help establish a training centre. His family's security demanded that there be utmost secrecy on the nature of his mission. He also told her that he would occasionally call her but to expect such calls from unregistered phone numbers.

He pondered too on his mission. Failure was not an option for him even to contemplate, given the mounting evidence of foreign militancy and terrorism in the state since his arrival. The insurgents, with their deviant brand of ideology and now led by an ISIS strongman, would in no time radicalize the unsuspecting population in matters of their faith. That would set the country backwards on a hate-filled and non-progressive path, something he would fight tooth and nail to prevent. It was a dangerous mission that he had undertaken. There was no guarantee that he or any one of his team members would not face injuries or even death. The kidnapping of Su Eng and what her fate would be at the hands of her captives weighed heavily on his head. The strategy and execution of their actions had, therefore, to be thorough and precise. The responsibility for that sat squarely on his shoulders.

The pahlwans noticed Zain's pensive mood. Sungkiah was the first to comment on it at their mid-morning coffee break the next day.

"The success of this mission must be weighing heavily on him," she observed.

"That of course, but more specifically, his constant worry may be about ensuring our safety in this adventure," said Azlan.

"It's a risky mission alright, but one can only die once, and if that is in the service of the nation, nothing could be more satisfying," remarked Sungkiah, to which there were nods all around.

"But with one qualification, if I go down it will have to be in the company of a dozen or more of my enemies," said Samy with a determined look in his eyes.

"Guys, we need to spare a thought too about our families. You think they'll buy fully into the patriotism stuff?" asked Dhanyal.

There was a wall of silence until a voice broke into their midst. It was Zain who had just then decided to join them. "Our fight here is as much for the safety of our families as that of the nation. We happen to be just in the front line. If we fail, there will be others, but then it will be a scaled-up confrontation for them. Stuffing out a threat that can spell doom for our country and well before it takes root is an option that doesn't often present itself. We must consider ourselves privileged for being chosen to undertake this task. Our only regret is that the secrecy of our mission bars us from confiding in our loved ones."

"You're dead right, boss. But I'm sure our families will share in a greater measure the pride of our nation in us if we succeed, even if some of us lose our lives in this mission. We're with you all the way, sir," said Kamal. The pahlawans all stood up to clap as Zain left them somewhat teary-eyed.

The scouting group that set out for the Kabili-Sepilok Forest Reserve on Sunday morning was split into two teams. The army team was assigned by Zain to check out the land access to the clandestine camp, starting from the Sepilok Jungle Resort. They were joined by the forest ranger, also dressed as a tourist. The car ride to the jungle resort located southeast took them barely 15 minutes.

Arriving at the jungle resort, the forest ranger revealed to the army team two unlisted meandering trails that led from the jungle resort to the interior of the jungle well behind the orangutan sanctuary.

The leader of the army team, who had a map in his hands, wanted to know whether there were trails that led from the Sepilok Forest Reserve directly south to areas behind the orangutan sanctuary as well. The question was a legitimate one, as this would provide for a two-pronged attack of the camp.

The forest ranger said he was not aware of any, but was confident of crafting one after studying the topography of the place.

The team decided to explore each of the unlisted trails from the jungle resort in turn; the cover the trails afforded both for entry and retreat were paramount to their assessment.

Zain, on the other hand, not wanting to discount possible riverine access to the camp, decided to hire a motorboat and go on an exploratory drive with his pahlawans on the Kabili River that ran through the jungle. They planned for two stopovers en route to the Kabili River – one was at Kampung Bambangan, and the other at the Sepilok Laut Reception Centre, accessed by the river Sungai Sepilok Kecil. They found it would take around four hours to walk to the Sepilok Jungle Resort from the village, but there was also car access which would take only about 20 minutes. In contrast, one could reach the jungle resort from Sepilok Laut by foot within 10 minutes.

Going upstream on the Kabili River meant meandering through mangrove forests into a wilderness area. Guided by GPS, they anchored the boat at a point and made their way inland. It was rough going in the virgin jungle that was unwelcoming of their intrusion.

An hour into the trek Zain called off their hike for the day. The approach did not seem practical for staging a stealth attack, let alone for a rushed retreat compared to the Sepilok Laut option.

After hearing the briefings by both teams, the meeting on Monday decided on a two-pronged attack, one starting from the Sepilok Forest Reserve, on a trail to be determined, and the other from Sepilok Laut, which would take one of the unlisted trails originating from the Sepilok Jungle Resort. Transport to Sepilok Laut would be by boat, while that to the Sepilok Forest Reserve would be by helicopter drop.

The modus operandi planned was that a six-person team would be engaged in each of the assaults, with the army taking up the frontal attack from the jungle resort end and Zain's pahlawans the rear attack from the Sepilok Forest Reserve end. Presented with the aerial photographs of the terrain of the large swathe of land covering the area from the Sepilok Forest to the south of the orangutan sanctuary, the forest ranger charted out a route to the enemy camp for study by the group.

Zain studied the proposed route carefully. "Yours is a virgin route, currently non-existent. Are you asking us to hack out this path as we head in the direction of the camp? No way! This has to be done without arousing suspicion several days ahead of the planned assault, and up to at least half a kilometre or so from the camp. A recce must also be made to ascertain whether there are barbed-wire entanglements and mines hidden along the edge of the jungle, and also any observation-posts up on trees. Can you handle all these with helpers that we can provide?" asked Zain of the forest ranger.

"No problem, sir. This can be done well within a few days," replied the ranger

"What we are still unsure of is how long it would take us before we get the first sight of the camp and approach it undetected to within 200 metres of it," said Dhanyal, looking in the direction of the forest ranger.

"Maximally an hour from either direction, I think," replied the ranger.

"In that case, the first team that arrives should message or talk to the other. We shall add satellite capability to all your iPhones if you don't have it already so that you can communicate in the jungle environment," chipped in the general.

"Are you planning a night raid or a daylight raid?" asked SAC Arshad.

"Not knowing the strength of our enemy, my gut feeling is to launch a night raid," opined Zain.

"That's settled then," said the general. "We shall plan for a night raid six days from today, starting from the respective starting points, at 1900 hours. You are all well-versed in what to carry with you, so I'm not going to advise you on it." He paused, struck by a sudden thought. Turning to Zain, he asked, "The cargo of firearms taken from the raided factory - can you tell us exactly what they were and their respective numbers?"

"There were in all three dozen semi-automatic AR-15 assault rifles, with the capability of firing 45 rounds per minute, and a large number of bullets, all packed into two boxes that we had previously tagged," replied Zain.

"I guess then that there might be around 40 insurgents in their camp, most of whom could be new recruits. Even so, I hope you will all be better equipped for your strike, with bulletproof jackets, M-16 Colt rifles, and RPGs supplied by our army camp. The latest drone pictures of the camp area 24 hours before the assault will be sent to your phones. Also, for your information, a police contingent with some paramedics will be on standby at Sepilok Laut from 8.00 p.m. onwards on that day. Let's go kick their asses, shall we?"

A large cry of Aye! greeted the general's concluding remark.

CHAPTER 18

*W*ith six days to pass before they staged their commando operation, the pahlawans were wondering what they might do in the meanwhile when Samy received a call from Anton. He instantly put his phone on speaker mode.

"Anton here, sir. The goods I have ordered from the Philippines have arrived in Tawau and are at my longhouse near the jetty. I suppose you want to inspect our packing of them before despatch to my clients."

"Of course! We shall head there tomorrow morning. I suppose some of that stuff would have been for Imran. Keep those aside for a moment. We shall see you then," replied Samy, and put the phone down.

"Sungkiah, since you have been there previously, you might as well take your team down there again. Those who might come to collect the cargo may not be Anton's real clients or middlemen. If that is the case, you might want to trail their vehicle. Also, ensure you get the phone numbers of Anton's clients. It may well be that the cargo is finally headed for Pulau Sebatik," said Zain.

"So, you don't want them to capture the clients or middlemen with the cargo of firearms, and let the cargo slip through to the terror cell?" asked Sungkiah.

"That's the sure-fire way to locate their hideouts and to capture their masterminds. Without weapons, the cells cannot function. The clients and middlemen can always be pulled up later," replied Zain.

As Zain had anticipated, among the men who came to collect the cargo, no face struck Anton as being familiar. One among them, authorized to check and receive the consignment, entered the longhouse, instructing the others to wait outside. He inspected the items packed in two boxes, cross-checking them with the listing in the delivery order that Azlan, who was in overalls, had handed him. Once the boxes were closed, he summoned his helpers to load them onto their waiting vehicle. It was then that Azlan spotted the fruit vendor from Kampung Attap Tengah among the helpers. Fortunately for Azlan, the fruit vendor did not recognize him. Upon getting the delivery order and the signed delivery receipt back from the man, Azlan gifted him with a key chain. In reality, it was a micro recorder.

Moments after they had left, the PP1 team was already on their trail. To Sungkiah's surprise, the vehicle stopped for delivery at the same double-storey shop lot that she had once entered. The vehicle then moved away. Sitting in their car, Sungkiah and her team listened in on the conversation.

The parties had opened the boxes and were inspecting the items, which included assault rifles equipped with telescopic optics, rocket-propelled grenade launchers, and ammunition.

"These are all top class; must have cost the boss a bomb," quipped one of them, which elicited laughter all around.

"Hope they know how to use these properly," said another.

"Don't worry, our trainers are past masters at handling these. Our boss has seen to that. I believe he has gone to meet the Sheikh," said the first speaker.

"And where is that?" asked an inquisitive member.

"No one knows, as he moves around, and electronic communication is taboo with him. The authorities, we were warned, have launched a manhunt for him. So, we have been asked not to refer to him as Sheikh anymore, but as *mudarison* ("teacher" in Arabic)," replied a new, stern voice. He paused a moment before continuing. "Let's close up the boxes. We have instructions someone will come and collect them in a few days."

Sungkiah and her team upon hearing the conversation wondered who their moneyed boss was.

"Why don't we check with Anton?" asked Dhanyal.

"Yes, of course," replied Sungkiah who immediately contacted Anton.

"I honestly do not know. All the people I met were the ones who were handling the request. Since you ask, I suspect they were acting on behalf of someone who wanted to keep himself in the background," was Anton's reply.

"Let's head back. There's nothing more we can do here if we're not to bust in on these guys for the present," said Dhanyal.

"Not yet. There's one pending matter. Zain had quietly asked me to confront Anton about his presence on the speedboat on the Kinabatangan River after he had discharged his schedule of delivery orders for the day," said Sungkiah.

Anton was still at his longhouse when the PP1 team went back. Shock registered on Anton's face when Sungkiah raised the question. It took him a few moments to reply.

"I was in the boat with my relatives. One of them wasn't feeling well, so we had to rush back."

"You sure about that? We have pictures of all those who were on board."

Beads of sweat began to appear on Anton's forehead. "Actually, I was holding back orders of firearms that were long overdue. They threatened to kill me if I didn't go along with the supply and let them test the guns in the quiet jungle environment. I had no choice."

"If that's true, you should have contacted us first. I want the full details of this group. This very moment! Who are they? Insurgents or those fronting for them? Where are they holding the guns you supplied them? The location of their terrorist camps. Leave nothing out. You're as good as dead if you lie. The same fate awaits you if we fail subsequently to trace the group. I'm now going to get my boss on the line on the speakerphone."

Anton sank into a chair in a heap, while Sungkiah dialled Zain. The phone interrogation lasted some twenty minutes. It became clear that the group was servicing many jungle hideouts of insurgents and operating from Sunga-Sungai. Pleased with Anton's disclosure, Zain asked Sungkiah to spare the man further harassment and to rush back to Ghosthouse.

Suddenly, seized by a devious thought, Sungkiah showed Anton the picture that Nasri had sent him of those who had come to recruit his village lads. Anton pointed to a bald man in the picture. "He was in the boat with others," declared Anton. The information was promptly passed on to Zain.

"Good. I'm leaving you now. Remember what I said. You will not be spared either by us or them if you decide to squeal," were Sungkiah's parting words to Anton as she and the pahlawans left the scene.

Dhanyal, who was at the wheel of their car, uncharacteristically speeded on the road, only to make a U-turn a short distance later to announce, "The new route I'm about to take passes through a McDonald's drive-thru. Is that OK?" Sungkiah and Azlan giggled loudly in agreement.

Upon their arrival at Ghosthouse, the PP1 team found Zain and the other pahlawans in animated conversation huddled over a large map of the area around Sungai-Sungai. They were discussing strategies to destroy the resource centre there that Anton had disclosed, which catered for terror cells in supplying firearms and asset recruitment.

"We need to identify the place first. Anton said he had never been to the place, but he recalled once being asked whether he could dispatch a batch of supplies to a shop lot near to a secondary school there, but the idea was dropped. We have little choice but to do a recce. Perhaps just two of us should go. A large group would arouse suspicion," said Zain.

"Samy's presence would also arouse instant ethnic curiosity," observed Kamal to laughter from the pahlawans.

"I volunteer to go with Azlan."

"OK, it's settled then. The trip will take you close to 4 hours. Interestingly, this place takes only half that time to reach if you set out from Pulau Jambongan. That should give you all food for thought," said Zain.

Early next morning saw Azlan and Kamal making the trip. They decided to masquerade as health officers checking for mosquito breeding sites at the suggestion of Azlan, who had played that role earlier. Luckily for them, their task was lightened by the presence in the town of just one main road with double-storey shop lots flanking both sides. Each of them handled one side of the road. Entering the large shop lot at the end of the road on his side, Azlan noted two security guards posted inside the building just past the entry door. He went in and donned his video camera sunglasses. There were some potted plants inside the building on both floors. He pretended to examine the plants in some detail. A cursory examination would have given him away as he saw there were CCTV installations. On the upper floor, his searching eyes spotted large unopened boxes arranged against the walls of two inner rooms. He guessed that they might contain firearms. There were over a dozen people in the area, including the bald man that Anton had identified, working at computers. Just then, two men entered the shop lot with a group of youngsters who were all ushered into a large room. Azlan surmised a video viewing was taking place in the room from the sounds that came through the partially open door. Convinced that this was the hideout they were seeking, he walked away from the place, giving the thumbs-up sign to the guards. Contacting Kamal, both assessed that a raid on the premises would present no problems.

Returning to Ghosthouse, the pahlawans set out in full force the following morning for a lightning raid. They had only the same two guards to silence, but they didn't anticipate the presence of a visitor on the upper floor who was then loading the new AR-15 rifle he had picked from the pile placed in front of him. At the sound of the pahlawans rushing up the stairs, the man instinctively disengaged the safety and turned around. Seeing them, the man fired his rifle through the glass door of his room, bringing down both Azlan and Dhanyal. But Sungkiah who was following behind felled the man with a clean shot that smashed into his skull. The others in the building offered no resistance. They were all caught by surprise, and none of them had guns in their possession to pose any threat.

The pahlawans were relieved that the shots fired at Azlan and Dhanyal had only winded them; the bullet-proof vests they were wearing had saved them. Zain caught the two kingpins who were running the resource centre and dragged them into one of the rooms for interrogation. They prised out of them the locations of terror cells they had dealings with and confiscated documents of illegal transactions in their possession. They also confiscated three computers they found in the place. Zain then informed Arshad of the successful raid and the evidence in his possession and left it to him to alert the local police to take custody of the prisoners.

"Congratulations! Looks like you have cut off a major supply line to militant groups. A great setback for the enemy but a priceless victory for us" responded Arshad. "Is today's raid, by any chance, some sort of a rehearsal for the main event?" he then asked in a quieter voice.

"Ha-ha. The opportunity came out of the blue, and we had to act quickly before they moved away. The raid we're jointly planning won't be as easy as this," replied Zain.

The following day, the pahlawans found themselves virtually confined indoors as technicians were wiring their place for remote closed-circuit television surveillance.

As the 'D-day' dawned for the assault on Saadam's terror cell, both teams were at their respective starting points precisely at the pre-determined hour. At the army camp meeting a day before the strike, Zain, along with all the pahlawans of groups PP1 and PP2, had received their jungle outfits, as well as instruction on the use of the firearms they were supplied with.

It was a precision raid. Both teams converged on the terrorist camp within the agreed distance of 100 metres before they communicated with each other. The time on Zain's watch showed 9.55 p.m. Stray barks from dogs in the camp were heard, but these raised no alarm in the camp. With the signal to move, both teams inched their way closer to the camp. Two makeshift palm-leaf huts were facing each other, one being smaller than the other, and 30 metres distant; their front and back portions were lighted by hanging bulbs on tree branches. Zain located Su Eng's position in the smaller hut and quickly apprised Samy and Sungkiah. A fenced pen between the huts with a tarpaulin-covered roof was where the dogs were placed. A distinct hum was in the air, which suggested that a gen-set was in operation. An enclosed area adjacent to the smaller hut hinted that it was probably where the gen-set was situated. They could see four sentries doing the rounds and cursing the dogs, which occasionally barked at them as they passed the pen.

They positioned themselves to shoot the sentries with silencers on their guns. Receiving the signal from Zain, they fired their shots simultaneously. All four of them fell to the ground, but there was no stir inside the huts. A walkie-talkie carried by one of the sentries suddenly came alive with a voice enquiring whether all was well. It remained unanswered, which drew three men out of the smaller hut with guns in their hands. One of them spotted the body of a sentry. Raising an alarm, all three men dashed back to the cover of the hut.

"Damn!" swore Zain under his breath as he fired an RPG at the gen-set housing. Pitch-darkness instantly covered the whole area. Another RPG aimed at the larger hut followed suit. The army team reacted quickly by firing an RPG on the second hut. Contending with flames and smoke, the two teams rushed in with guns blazing towards the huts before the insurgents could come out in their numbers.

Zain, Azlan and Dhanyal went in for a frontal attack on the larger hut, while Samy and Sungkiah headed towards the smaller hut. The initial spray of bullets randomly fired in all directions by Zain and his pahlawans upon rushing into the huts brought down several of the insurgents. The suddenness of the attack had caught the enemy off guard.

The huts were in darkness in most places, but enveloping flames and smoke brought on by the grenade explosion soon saw many insurgents rushing out from the other rooms. The pahlawans carrying their switched-on weapon-mounted lights easily targeted the armed insurgents. In the melee in the larger hut, Zain spotted Saadam firing his gun while retreating. He shot the gun out of the ISIS headman's hand with his pistol, and both he and Azlan cornered and captured him before he could react further.

Samy and Sungkiah, following their initial rush into the smaller hut, quickly retreated to the back of the hut with the approach of the army team. They gunned down all the armed insurgents who were initially rushing to make a quick getaway at the back of the hut. But then, as many unarmed insurgents started coming out, Samy allowed Sungkiah, with protective cover, to enter the back of the hut in search of Su Eng. He soon followed. They found her gagged and tied up between a pile of boxes. She was bleeding in both her hands. Sungkiah rushed to free her. Within moments Samy lifted her out of the hut and they brought her to safety. Sungkiah stayed back to attend to Su Eng, while Samy rushed to join the other pahlwans and signal her safe rescue.

The militants in the larger hut, seeing Saadam captured, laid down their arms. Azlan and Zain brought him out into the open area between the huts with his hands cuffed at his back.

But then an unexpected thing happened. One of the insurgents wearing a suicide bomb vest came out of nowhere and was menacingly moving towards Saadam, holding what looked like a triggering device in his hand. He appeared ready to blow himself up with his mentor rather than allow their capture by kafirs (infidels). He shouted to his attackers to lay down their arms or face the risk of being blown to bits. He was held back at gunpoint about 3 to 4 yards from Saadam by Samy, who in the process raised his left thumb above his head. Zain instantly interpreted Samy's signal to mean Su Eng was rescued, but could not quite heave a sigh of relief, for the situation unfolding before him was of nightmarish proportions. The man had visibly packed his body with explosives that could bring many down. Zain had been tasked to bring Saadam back alive but he had not anticipated this out-of-the-blue situation. He quickly ordered the pahlawans to retreat while he and Azlan stood their ground on either side of Saadam. Azlan, flanking Saadam on the right, then made a strategic move. Going behind Zain, he whispered "Both of you turn around with your backs to the woods where I'm now going."

With the retreat of Samy and Azlan, the suicide bomber ventured closer to Saadam. But he hadn't counted on Azlan taking up a position quickly behind the trees and following his movement through the telescopic sight on his M-16 rifle. As Azlan had anticipated, the man slowly approached Saadam on the side he had just vacated. The man's left arm was free, but not his right, which presumably held the triggering device. Azlan waited until the man's right hand came clearly into his line of fire. Optical zooming revealed that the man had his right thumb drawn in, presumably resting on a push button or switch. He knew he had just one chance to hit the man's wrist. And he was spot-on. With the one-shot, the suicide bomber instantly released the device, which fell harmlessly to the ground. Another bullet aimed at the man's forehead fell him backwards.

Dhanyal, unaware of Azlan's moves but sensing the gravity of the situation, decided to video shoot the event unfolding before his eyes. The light from the flames engulfing one of the huts was bright enough for him to record the video on his cell phone. He was not to know this, but the video was a vital record of the excruciating moments of Saadam's capture that hit the national and foreign television networks the next day.

Members of the army team witnessing the scene from the other hut rushed forward to surround the insurgents who were trying to sneak away into the woods. And so also Zain's pahlawans once they came out of their initial shock. Azlan was the toast of the two teams.

The prisoners were all bound and placed at the centre of the courtyard facing the two huts, with the wounded and dead segregated. Members of Zain's team sustained no injuries; the army team registered a couple of casualties but nothing major. Medical personnel from the army attended to all the wounded, including the insurgents. Su Eng, who had sustained abrasion injuries on her hands, also received treatment from them. She appeared frail and dehydrated. She was hugged warmly by all her teammates.

Saadam had his clothes brusquely searched for hidden cyanide pills, but there was none. Kamal and Samy then placed a hood over his head and rained a few blows upon his head and body. No whimper, no sound came from Saadam. A restraining hand from Kamal held back Samy, who looked set to deliver a fresh round of punches. "We don't want to have his face badly disfigured for a photograph," explained Kamal. Samy, steeped in anger, contended himself hurling a few verbal insults at the man in both Tamil and English before moving away, just as when Sungkiah came on the scene.

"What was all that about?" she enquired of Kamal.

"Oh, he was upset he couldn't get the man here to groan with his initial punches," said Kamal. He then added with a twinkle in his eye, "*Elok kita berbual dalam Bahasa kita*" (Best we talk in our language). Sungkiah understood what he meant, and the rest of their short conversation was in the vernacular.

"He seems to have an unforgiving nature when dealing with bad boys," observed Sungkiah.

"I don't blame him. He was only a young kid on an estate when his father was killed in a drunken brawl. The family had to struggle, but it was a conscious decision on his part when he came of age to join the police force. He finds solace in punishing miscreants of the law and those who show no value for life. Speaking of life, I owe mine to him for his valour at Jambongan," replied Kamal.

"You have not worked together before this mission?"

"Not really. I was in the police field force along with Zain, while Samy was in the crime branch. We met two years ago in Kota Kinabalu when we both attended a virtual-reality- based counter-terrorism course."

"Must have been an interesting course."

"It certainly was. It's really an amazing experience with the headgear you put on."

"And Azlan?"

"We met only at Terendak. He is more composed than Samy. You would have noticed he's good with guns and the other gadgets we carry. I suppose that's on account of his diploma in engineering background. His father was with the police. That must have motivated him to join the force."

A while later saw Zain moving up to Saadam. Removing the hood, he looked straight into the man's somewhat bruised face and asked, "So, you have sent for your Afghani comrade to join you?" Saadam's eyes, which were roving aimlessly, went fleetingly on a hold, enough for Zain to infer that it was indeed the case. Zain then made him squat on the ground along with the other prisoners.

The news of Saadam's capture was conveyed by Zain first to Brigadier General Othman. "*Syabas*! This is the news I have been waiting for", the general exulted. He immediately ordered police reinforcements to the camp to bring back the prisoners and the seized weapons. He also dispatched two helicopters to the Sepilok Forest Reserve to be in waiting; one to pick up the two commando teams and their prized captive, and the other to bring in the wounded.

CHAPTER 19

*T*he news of Saadam's capture gripped the interest of the nation for much of the week and more, but Zain knew that the fight with ISIS in the state was far from over. He had alerted SCSC on the impending arrival in Sabah of Saadam's ally from Afghanistan, and their response had been to beef up security at all entry points into the state and increase vigilance on the coast through more frequent boat patrols and use of drones. The news about Saadam's ally was not released to the media.

On the fifth day into Saadam's capture, the militants reacted to show their defiance. Mortar shells were fired on two government buildings, one each in Sandakan and Tawau, and car bombs exploded in five townships across the state, causing extensive damage to property and wounding scores of citizens. Fortunately, no deaths were reported. But the impudence of the attack revealed that the insurgents were moving in freely among the masses undetected and were not just confined to terror cells.

The following day saw General Ghazali Abu Hassan of the Joint Forces Command flying down to Lahad Datuk. He had convened an urgent meeting of SCSC and wanted all the top brass of security operations in the state to be present. Zain was invited to the meeting.

"Ladies and gentlemen, you can guess why I'm here," began the general. "Let me at the outset congratulate the two teams that captured alive the ISIS leader Saadam. His capture will considerably slow down the activities of the militants, despite the bravado they put up yesterday. This brings me to the point I raised several months back in KL. That is, we need more action on the ground to pick out their hiding places in the urban areas and also identify their erstwhile supporters. I see that Sandakan and Tawau appear to be their favourite operational zones. I'm authorizing a joint police-army flush-out operation of all insurgents and suspects in these two townships. I want the fingers of fear to penetrate the minds of those who are abetting the insurgents. Apply curfew in sectoral areas in these towns before you embark on a house-to-house search. This may cause dissent among a portion of the population, but their safety is paramount. You may recall we had to exercise similar steps during the Communist insurgency in Peninsular Malaysia. Track all leads you can get on the clandestine trafficking and production of weapons and IEDs. I expect to see positive results within a couple of months."

It was a stern message. The discussion that followed centred essentially on requirements to beef up security both inland and at the coast, in particular, the need to establish more police and army posts and the provision of aerial support in the form of drones and surveillance aircraft, to all of which the general promised prompt action.

The general sought out Zain at the close of the meeting. "That was a job well done, tracking the whereabouts of the man and then capturing him. Othman filled me in on the details. Also, how you delivered Mario, who had escaped our clutches and helped bring to book some money launderers who might be the source of funds for the militants. I'm impressed."

"Thank you, General. Luck and technology have played a part in this. We are now after the middlemen who have been involved in supplying weapons to the militants. But the game is not over. You might have heard, General, that Saadam's assistant from Afghanistan is trying to make his way here from North Kalimantan "

"What?" interrupted the general. "That's news to me. Why was I not alerted on this?"

"It is not a confirmed piece of news yet, General. Perhaps you might want to check it out with the CIA. When I questioned Saadam about it, I noticed a slight change on his otherwise poker face, which makes me think there is some truth in the rumour," replied Zain.

"I see," remarked the general. "Keep up the good work."

Zain came away from the meeting convinced that he and his teams were on the right track in pursuing the intelligence they had stumbled upon or traced through intercepted phone messages. He now had to push Brigadier

General Othman for the drone flights over Golong and Pulau Sebatik. Perhaps also to reach out to the two CIA agents for complementary satellite imagery.

The next two weeks saw the pahlawans tracking and capturing the middlemen in arms trafficking whose names Anton and Imran had provided. One name which was missing was that of the elusive "boss" whose underlings had collected the weapons cargo at Tawau.

"I guess the time has come to undertake a second round of surveys with split teams," remarked Zain after the roundup of the known middlemen was completed. "Sungkiah, the Tawau job is for you and Azlan. Kamal and Samy can search the area around Golong. Dhanyal and Su Eng will revisit Pulau Sebatik to check on any new happenings there, and I shall go with them. As there are only two cars, the Pulau Sebatik group will hitch a ride in Sungkiah's car to Tawau and hire a car from there to move around. We all should stay in the same hotel in Tawau town. We shall all leave tomorrow. Let's keep our ears to the ground, and see what's brewing out there."

Arriving at the shop lot in Tawau after checking in at their hotel, Sungkiah and Azlan parked their car opposite the building. She dialled Anton and asked him to call the person whom he had previously visited in the building to tip him off that some customs officers were on their way to the building and to hide all weapons in his possession.

Within moments, the pahlawans saw two men coming out carrying a box which they placed in the car which was stationed near the front of the building. As they retreated into the building, Azlan sprinted across the road to place a magnetic GPS tracking device between the car's rear-wheel and exhaust. The men reappeared with a second box and yet another before they sped away.

About ten minutes after the car's departure, Azlan and Sungkiah entered the building and went straight to the upper floor, where they burst into the office on a pretext of a lightning raid. Other than a lady receptionist, there were four men in the office. Azlan asked the receptionist to leave the building immediately. Announcing their intentions, the pahlawans then went about their search, peering here and there, before descending on the files. Sungkiah stood aloof, studying the environment around her that might surreptitiously be hiding some gunmen. She didn't spot any. She summoned the four men to sit with her and asked to see their phones. In one, he saw the call that Anton had made. She kept the phones near her, and point-blank asked, "Who's your boss?"

The senior man among them nodded. Sungkiah knew that this was not the man Anton had contacted. They were covering up for someone, but she persisted. "I mean, who's the real owner of this import-export business that you conduct here. The silent partner whose name is not on the records, but who finances the operations?"

The senior man scoffed. "The real owner? We're all the partners that there are."

Sungkiah leaned forward and smacked the man on his face. She then drew out her gun.

"We shall beat the pulp out of you all if you don't give us the answer. The alternative is to shoot you all dead, which will be legitimate as you are trafficking in guns, which carries a death penalty if you are caught possessing them. You just arranged for three boxes to be carried into your car, didn't you?" asked Sungkiah.

The men were speechless. They never before had faced a menacing female investigator, and looked terrified. She separated them from each other to four corners of the office. "You will whisper the name of your boss to my colleague here when he comes to you. If we find any variation in the answer, that person will be shot dead. Is that clear?"

Their answer was unanimous. It was the name of a high-ranking state assemblyman who hailed from Tawau – Datuk Adnan.

With Azlan at her side, Sungkiah then ordered the senior man to bring out the files on the transactions of armaments and other illicit items. In one invoice, Azlan saw cigars were listed. He recalled being briefed once how hollowed-out cigars could be used to pack in marijuana. He turned to the men and noted innocently,

"So you import cigars besides guns? Get me one, now. I don't mind smoking one."

One of the men obliged, bringing out a pack from a set of drawers. Azlan withdrew one and with a pencil, pushed out its contents. It was not all tobacco. A whitish powder appeared to be mixed with it. He was certain it was a drug.

Sungkiah then went outside and contacted ACP Rosmah Binti Yahaya, informing her in some detail about the sleeper cell and the combined gun and drug trafficking business that the company was engaged in. The police arrived quickly on the scene. Sungkiah gave them the GPS location of the vehicle with the hidden guns.

Meeting Zain later at the hotel, Sungkiah gave him a detailed account of the sleeper cell that she and Azlan had exposed. Zain was elated at hearing the news. The revelation about the assemblyman was the first concrete evidence of there being political and financial patronage for the militants. "There could well be others," he mused to Sungkiah. "This has to be delicately handled. I shall have to inform Datuk Azhari about this."

"We have no direct evidence of the man's contact with the militants. He could claim ignorance of owning the company, or if he did, he could feign ignorance of the illegal side activities his subordinates have been doing.

"Why not alert the local police or SCSC?" she asked.

"Political pressure most likely will be exerted on the local police to drop the investigation. We need to invoke the probe at the federal level involving Bukit Aman, and the best route for this is through Datuk Azhari. The documents you have confiscated from their office will prove to be vital. Who knows? This man could be a client of either the accounting firm or the commercial law firm in Tawau, both of which we know are already on Bank Negara's blacklist for money laundering. I may have to hint that to Datuk Azhari," replied Zain.

Zain then resolved that all the pahlawans at Tawau should descend on Pulau Sebatik. "We need to do some serious scouting work near the island's shared border with Indonesia.

Arriving at the Batu-Batu jetty, Dhanyal went around to find a large motorboat they could charter for a day.

"I'm sure that if Saadam's man has indeed set foot in North Kalimantan, it could only be with the help of the ISIS-linked Jemaah Ansharut Daulah group. To reach our shores unseen by boat, they would probably arrange for his exit from Nunukan or the Tarakan Islands to their end of Sebatik Island. He would then attempt to cross over the border. Perhaps there may be no cross-over at all, if he aims to establish a terror cell on the Indonesian side with recruits drawn in from both countries. It's a frightening thought," said Zain to the rest of the group who were huddled together.

"Maybe a border wall, just like what has been built along the US-Mexican border is what we might need," said Azlan, eliciting laughter all around.

"Without drones being called into play, it's going to be a difficult task for us. Are you still in touch with your CIA contacts?" asked Sungkiah, looking at Zain.

Just then her mobile phone came alive with an alert sign. She turned to Zain excitedly. "Looks like our village lads are on the move."

"Call Dhanyal back. We will take the boat later. I want to know where they are headed," said Zain, leading the pack to a new roadside coffee shop at the waterfront area.

Sipping his Hailam coffee, Zain contacted Jack of the CIA duo.

"Hello, Jack! I didn't get the chance to thank you both for getting me to the hospital the other day after the shootout. You had already left when I came out of the treatment room."

"Oh, that was nothing. We had to leave because the police were around. Incidentally, we heard the wonderful news of the capture of Saadam. We presume you had a major hand in it. Congrats!" said Jack, who appeared to be genuinely pleased.

"Thank you. My team, along with another from the army, staged a two-pronged attack on the place. I must say that your satellite imagery, along with some drone pictures, helped us to pinpoint the hideout. I have, of course, kept our meeting secret. Only members of my team know that you exist."

"That's good. Once our cover is blown, we'd be dead ducks."

"Jack, I might need your help again with the satellite imagery for another venue, if that's possible. It is Pulau Sebatik, which lies just off Tawau. The island shares a long and porous land boundary with Indonesia. I have this gut feeling that militants might have set up one or more terror cells in the heavily forested sections at the boundary belt. The border's coordinates are 4° 10' N and 117° 47' E. I wonder if you can get me some views along this border."

"Wow, you guys are certainly on the move! No problem. We'll look for them. Hope to send you some images later in the day."

An hour elapsed, and Sungkiah's suspicions grew stronger that the village lads were indeed being brought towards the ferry terminal. "Some of them might identify us if we go back to the terminal. Chances are they might not then take the ferry, and would hire boats instead to get to the island."

"We have little choice but to wait. With our binoculars, we can easily see which section of the island they would be heading for. Just be on the lookout for their arrival, and see whether all of them who alight are taking the trip. Those that remain behind may be their spies whom we have to give the slip – the hard way, if necessary. In any case, charter a boat in advance, if you must. We shall board it at the opportune time," said Zain, radiating a big smile.

An hour further in waiting, the pahlawans finally saw the village recruits alighting from two taxis, led by three well-bodied men. Dhanyal surreptitiously captured them on video using his cell phone as they headed for the terminal. As anticipated, they got into two speedboats to take them across to the island. The boats steered past the farthest east end of the island towards the direction of Wallace Bay before disappearing from view.

Zain ordered his men to get their rucksacks out of their cars. "We may have to brave the night in the jungle," he warned the pahlawans as they began their pursuit, with Dhanyal piloting their chartered motorboat.

As they were nearing one of the bends on the coast, they saw the two hired boats returning. Zain stopped one of them to enquire where they had dropped their customers, only to learn that it was a mere couple of nautical miles ahead. With his binoculars focussed on the beach, Zain signalled Dhanyal to slow down the boat and steer it toward the shore, where he had spotted empty drink cartons littered on the beach. They all alighted at the spot, and the men then carried the boat to the cover of trees and undergrowth.

The GPS tracker on Sungkiah's phone enabled them before long to identify the *jalan tikus* their adversary had taken. It bore the unmistakable stamp of novices brusquely disturbing the riotous lushness of growth along the path.

Going deeper in, the path became increasingly dark as the jungle canopy shrouded out most of the sunlight, but they trudged on, taking in the musky aroma of the jungle. They appeared to be proceeding in a north-westerly direction. They walked on for a couple of hours before they saw a clearing. It was obvious to all that the group ahead had rested there for a while, for there were plastic and paper wrappings strewn on the jungle floor along with food remnants that had attracted insects. A giant anteater fled the scene as they approached. Zain halted his group there as well for a short rest. The GPS tracker on Sungkiah's phone indicated that the adversaries were less than a mile ahead. Zain also noted from his phone that Jack had forwarded him some real-time satellite pictures.

"Incredible!" shouted Zain as he showed his team the images. "These shots are from outer space, and they show us trailing our adversary. Can you beat that? A cleared area with a dwelling is seen in the top corner of this image. It could well be their terror cell. Can we relate its coordinates with the international boundary line?"

"Let me try," responded Azlan, who then started working on the data. Minutes later, he had the answer.

"The dwelling is on the Indonesian side of the border some three kilometres in. We have to walk another nine kilometres or so to get there. That means easily another four hours or so of walking along this path."

"OK, let's push on then. We shall do a recce of their camp and place a couple of GPS tracking devices once we get there. We will then backtrack to our side of the border and then veer off the path a couple of kilometres to set up camp for the night."

Approaching the enemy camp, they found confirmation that it was a terror cell by the presence of black-and-white ISIS flags wound around trees all along the path. The camp had just one traditional longhouse with an antenna disc on its roof. An open well stood at one side of it. Fronting the house was a large cleared area at one end of which there were many rifle shooting targets. The entire area was barbed-wire fenced, with just the one sentry post entry. Several wooden bench seats adorned the front of the house at one end, and stacked alongside them were many foldable tables.

There was a flickering fire inside the compound close to the camp entrance to which the two guards appeared to be constantly drawn while manning the sentry post. Zain noticed there was a chill in the air. He and his team waited around the perimeter. They could see no sniper observation points on the roof of the building.

Suddenly, they heard the Maghrib prayers coming from inside the house. He signalled Azlan, Sungkiah, and Dhanyal to make their entry at the back of the house. They cut through the barbed wire and quickly sneaked in behind the building. It was a difficult task to peer into the house that was on stilts. Azlan had to be carried on the shoulders of Dhanyal to peer through some of the half-open windows. There were battery-operated LED lamps and kerosene lamps aplenty in the longhouse. The occupants were all congregated for prayer in the large vestibule; the remainder of the space in the longhouse had the customary arrangement of rooms flanking both sides of a central corridor. Azlan counted the numbers assembled for prayer; there were some thirty of them. Only a handful of them looked like Filipinos; the rest were a mix of Bugis and Bajau.

Peering next into one of the back rooms through a crack in the wall with the flashlight in his hands, he saw that it was their weapons room. There was a big cache of grenades, weapons, IED-making equipment, and booster charges for RPGs. Several partially assembled suicide vests were seen left on the floor.

The flashlight might have attracted attention, as he heard someone opening the creaky room door. In an instant, he switched off the light and looked at the figure standing in the doorway. The man lingered there for a moment before moving away. Azlan then retreated quickly with his team, but not before placing a GPS tracker device on the building. They had barely crossed the fencing when several of the men came rushing to the rear of the house. The sentries who were cosy at the fire were admonished for not taking turns to patrol the compound.

Zain and the pahlawans then retraced their steps to set up their night camp as planned on the Malaysian side of the border. They vacated the camp at the break of dawn to where they had hidden the motorboat. Their next destination was Kampung Haji Kuning. Azlan took over the control of the boat, being familiar with the sea and land route to the place.

At the back of Zain's mind was a nagging question; could there be a terror cell that was not hidden away but surreptitiously operating in front of their eyes? He wondered about the far reaches of Kampung Haji Kuning, which would fit the bill, as it was a village that appeared to accommodate illegals from Malaysia on a walk-in, walk-out basis. The satellite photographs had also captured this village. It was the most prominent among the few other scattered dwellings along the border.

They had a sumptuous breakfast upon arriving at the village via the *jalan tikus* pathway they had traversed before. They next went around the village outskirts to make discreet enquiries. The questions they posed to the villagers were direct, and so were the responses received.

Q: "Is there a lot of smuggling activity here?"

A: "Yes, it sure is big business. Many new arrivals here depend on it for their livelihood."

Q: "Are you in favour of an Islamic State?"

A: "We don't mind if this would address our economic needs as well."

Q: "If there is a call to arms to establish an Islamic State will you support it?"

A: "You mean militancy? No. we don't believe in violence."

Q: "Has anyone come around here to talk about it?"

A: "Some people have come, once in a way."

Although the village was in Indonesian territory, the affirmative answers to the first two questions worried the pahlawans immensely. While smuggling may seamlessly feed into other clandestine activities, the pro-Islamic State sentiments required only the seeds of coercion or indoctrination to manifest themselves more tangibly on the ground. The more he thought about it, the more convinced Zain was that the JAD had already earmarked the area as a base and would soon be actively involved there. The spill-over effects into Sabah could then be swift and severe.

CHAPTER 20

$\mathcal{K}$amal, Samy and Su Eng took almost four hours to get to Golong. Upon arrival there, they realised that the place was only a small township, with no stayover facilities in the form of hotels. The closest they could find was some 50 kilometres out of Golong. They failed to detect any response from the GPS tracking device they had placed in the weapons box that the insurgents had received through Mario's middlemen.

As far as they could discern from the road map, there was just the one side road leading to and from the Sapi-Nangoh Federal Highway to Golong, which sat at the edge of a virgin forest. But they couldn't discount the presence of several hidden jungle paths that led to the deeper sections of the surrounding jungle, or the entry provided by the meandering stream, Sungai Kaidangan. It was conceivable that the insurgents might have used any one of such routes.

"We need to check with the locals first thing in the morning if a group of men have recently gone into the jungle carting some goods," said Samy to Kamal after settling in at their lodge.

"Yup! We also need their assistance in showing us the hidden jungle paths. We have to pretend we're naturalists. For all you know, we may be able to find out if there also exists a *jalan tikus* leading to Jambongan Island."

"According to this map, there is an easier route to get to the island. We have to get back to the Sapi-Nangoh Federal Highway and move towards Pitas. Roughly 10 to 12 kilometres along this highway there is a side road that veers to the east as Jalan Pantai Delima. It looks like a dead-end road on the map. From there, Pulau Jambongan is even closer," Samy pointed out.

"We need to check that out. Also, whether there are regular police patrols on that stretch you mention, as I'm sure SCSC may have cast its security net across the island and a good portion of the mainland facing it as well. I wonder if Zain has managed to get drone surveillance of this area initiated."

"Speak of the devil, that's him on the line now," said Samy.

"Hello, Zain, we were just talking about you. Hope you have some news about drone assistance."

"I have reminded the general. Let me brief you on our visit to Pulau Sebatik," replied Zain.

When he had finished, it was Samy's turn to indicate to Zain their proposed surveillance plans on the hinterland of Golong and routes from there to Jambongan Island.

"That's good. They may be out there already sizing up a suitable place to set up their camp. It will take time for them to recruit and indoctrinate their members, but establishing the terror cell can, in the meanwhile, prove to be a haven for the JAD and Bangsamoro groups who are being hounded in their respective countries. We already have evidence of their movement from Turtle Islands and Pulau Sebatik. Let us know if you need our support out there," said Zain in closing.

The following morning the three pahlawans went out to talk to the locals to gather information. They learnt that there were two oft-used paths to the jungle when illegal logging was rampant; presently, only hunters used them for catching wild boars, monitor lizards, and civet cats. Also brought to their notice was a long-disused path towards the east of the town, once created by illegal loggers directionally towards Pulau Jambongan. But they could gain no information from the locals on whether some outsiders had recently entered the jungle through their town.

"To avoid identification, they must have perhaps entered the jungle environment by another path before reaching the town," observed Kamal.

"Maybe they brought along an inflatable boat to go up to Sungai Kaidangan with their cargo before veering into the jungle at some point," remarked Su Eng.

"You both may be right. We don't have an inflatable boat. So, let's do some scouting along the three-kilometre stretch of road that connects the town to the federal highway. We may encounter a trail or two leading to the jungle before we hit the river. Let's drive halfway back to the federal highway and start looking around there," said Samy.

They did exactly that and could not believe their luck when they noticed the sudden appearance of a motorbike coming out of the woods and heading towards Golong. They stopped the motorcyclist and asked him where in the jungle he had come from. He refused to answer until Samy brought out his gun and said they were plainclothes police.

"I just went to deliver food to a camp," was the man's reply.

"How far in? Is it a straight track?"

"About four kilometres. There is fork in the track at two places. Go left at the first fork, and right at the next."

"How many of them are there? Are you sure you are not dealing in drugs with them?"

"No, *tuan* (sir). I swear. There are ten of them."

"Are they armed? Do they look like foreigners?"

"Yes, tuan. They look like Filipinos."

"Do you have any of their contact numbers on your phone?"

"I don't have a phone, tuan."

"OK, leave your bike next to our car. You will come with us."

The frightened young man had little option but to comply. They followed the trail with the young man as their guide. When they reached some 10 metres from the camp, they halted and asked the young man to stay his ground behind a tree and not to run away at any cost. The surroundings were echoingly quiet. They saw a wooden hut with a thatched roof that appeared to have been newly erected. Situated between two big trees, it was a stone's throw away from a flowing stream behind it. Some men were busy erecting a barbed-wire fence around the camp's perimeter. They were unarmed. Samy counted four of them.

Motioning Kamal and Su Eng to storm the hut, Samy surprised the four men by rushing at them. No shots were fired. Almost simultaneously, Kamal and Su Eng barged into the hut with an initial burst of rifle fire. The remainder of the insurgents therein were completely caught off-guard and offered no resistance.

The prisoners were handcuffed and ordered to be seated on the floor of the hut. All their phones were confiscated.

Samy and Kamal had a quiet word among themselves before Samy turned to the prisoners.

"Who's your spokesman?"

Their heads turned to one man. Samy asked him to come forward.

"You speak English?"

"Yeah," replied the man

"We take it you are trying to establish a terror camp here. We could have you all shot and done with. Luckily for you, we're the auxiliary police, so we can be lenient if you play to our demands. By leniency, we mean we could have you all deported back to Mindanao without knowledge of the state security."

The spokesperson turned to speak to the others in Tagalog. Turning to Samy, he nodded.

"We demand answers to some questions: when are you expecting the arrival of your next batch of Bangsamoro comrades, and where are they going to land? Where is the new ISIS man presently? And can you give us the names of some of the high officials in Sabah who support your cause for separatism and an Islamic State?"

Samy's voice was stern as he spoke. No one moved, save for Su Eng, who was wielding her cell phone for a video shot of the proceedings.

The spokesperson turned again to face his comrades. They were engaged in an animated conversation. Kamal, who knew a smattering of Tagalog, heard one of the men saying, "Don't worry. They have no way of verifying what we say."

At this, Kamal turned to the prisoners. "By the way, my friend here has a short temper. The moment he suspects you are pulling a fast one, he will kill one amongst you instantly. And I suspect the person who just said that you could lie to us will be the one." A frightened whisper spread among them. They hadn't counted on their language understood by their captors.

The spokesperson finally found his voice. "Two batches are expected to land in four days. They will come by night by speedboat after getting off a trawler at sea.

One batch will head for the Turtle Islands, like we had come. Another batch will go to a village first on Jambongan Island, then make their way here." He paused. Samy didn't say a word but looked at the pahlawans, prompting Kamal to ask the man, "Where in Pulau Jambongan will they disembark, and where were you planning to meet up with them?"

"They will go ashore at a village. Some locals will bring them to Pitas, and we will fetch them from there," replied the man.

"What about the group landing in the Turtle Islands? Where are they headed?" Kamal pressed.

"Some forest reserve. I forget the name."

"Your answer to my other questions?" asked Samy.

"We do not know who or where the man from ISIS is. Our comrades in Indonesia are handling his trip. We do not know any high officials you mention. Only heard of one Tuan Sipil. We don't know where he is, but were told he will make special arrangements with the police and immigration to help us."

"Did you have any help getting here from the Turtle Islands?"

The man's head wagged back and forth before he said, "Yes, we traded our speedboat for the two fishing boats used by the boatmen who were waiting for us at sea off Sandakan."

Samy smiled at the response. He imagined the coast guards chasing the speedboat only to realise they were locals taking it for a spin.

"Have any of you contacted this man Sipil or any other locals since coming here?" asked Kamal.

"No one," replied the spokesman, shaking his head, as did the others.

Samy immediately pounced on the answer. "How did you get to the kampung at Pekan Beluran, then?"

"Oh, yes, tuan, I forgot. There was one contact number the boatmen gave us. It's in my phone. I contacted the man, and he gave us the directions to get to the kampung."

Samy retrieved the number and asked, "So you are expecting a call in four days on this phone from the new arrivals in Pulau Jambongan?"

The man nodded, his eyes flickering uneasily.

"You will be in our custody for a week while we verify all that you have said. For your sake, I hope you have told the truth," warned Samy as he went out to look for the young man behind the trees, and also to inform Zain of his captives.

"I guess we have little choice but to release the prisoners to the local police at Beluran and take SCSC into our confidence about the planned landings of the insurgents in Pulau Jambongan and the Turtle Islands. I feel that the initial landings should not be intercepted, as that's the only way we can seize the locals who are helping the insurgents. I shall have a word on this with General Othman. Leave this guy Sipil out of the picture for the moment, but all others who are caught in the net after the landing of the insurgents need to be grilled by us. Insist on that," was Zain's advice to Samy.

"In that case, we may have to get back to Beluran here for the interrogation. I want to gather as much information as possible on the locals who are behind the arrangements to bring in the new arrivals to Pitas," replied Samy, who was immensely satisfied by Zain's response.

General Othman, however, disagreed with Zain's suggestion of allowing the insurgents to escape capture immediately upon their entry into Sabah's territorial waters.

"Their arrivals are usually late at night, and it looks like this time they are coming in large numbers. They are, therefore, more likely to head for several destinations and not just the one, hoping to group later inland. It will be easier to catch them all at sea."

Zain appreciated his point of view. The insurgents duly arrived at the Turtle Islands only to be apprehended by the coast guard, who were waiting for them. However, no clandestine arrivals were observed on Jambongan Island. General Othman wondered whether the intelligence report was correct.

"Some alert must have gone out to them before they set out on their trip to the island," opined Zain. "Conceivably, they must have had an alternative plan, which might have been to head further south along the coast."

"It's difficult to imagine that, as the entire stretch of coast is under heavy surveillance. It's more probable they may have aborted their plans when they got wind of the failure of the Turtle Islands landings," remarked General Othman.

"More likely they have postponed their plans, sir. We cannot afford to lessen the frequency of our coastal patrols just yet," muttered Zain. His unspoken thoughts were, "*What if they did land unnoticed, perhaps a day earlier?*"

That amazing insight was indeed true. Under cover of night, some twenty insurgents wearing scuba diving outfits and clinging below two floating wooden platforms that resembled parts of a shipwrecked boat guided the platforms past the unsuspecting coast guard to the coastal village of Kampung Nibong. They were rebel soldiers who had left the all-Muslim unit of the Philippines Army to join BIFF, and had with them GPS and a range of espionage gadgetry. They went immediately into hiding in the village, awaiting favourable intelligence reports from their informers before making their move.

At the hands of Samy and Kamal, the network of locals with Sulu State or Islamic State leanings was scrutinized to a detail that had the local police in awe. Some corrupt members manning police posts in Beluran and Tawau were identified and slapped with immediate suspension and jail sentence terms under the Internal Security Act.

An overjoyed General Ghazali called to congratulate Zain and his pahlawans for foiling a major militant offensive that was on the cards. The occasion presented itself for Zain to request daily drone flypasts over Pulau Sebatik. It was instantly approved. And so was his request to interrogate the disloyal police who had been placed in custody, as he felt that they would not have dared to help the insurgents without orders from a higher police or political authority.

While his meetings with the police detainees in Tawau yielded no information on the elusive Sipil, he was in some luck when he arrived in Beluran town. One of the detainees recalled an official car drawing up in the middle of the night at his police beat base and delivering several gift baskets. He could not see the car's passengers, but noted that it had a Z number plate. Zain knew at once that it was an armed forces vehicle, but the answers to the 'who and why' questions concerning the gift deliveries evaded him. The more pressing question in his mind was whether the enemy had infiltrated army outposts as well, or was it just a ruse using an army number plate to avoid scrutiny by police at road checkpoints? The more he thought about it, the more convinced he was that it could be the latter. This would also explain why Sipil's movements had thus far failed to attract attention.

Acting on an impulse, Zain decided to make a random visit to a police beat base, accompanied by Sungkiah. He chose the one he had earlier seen at Sungai-Sungai. Arriving there, he soon realised the enormity of the duties of those manning the post to keep a vigil on illegal entries. He gathered that the police personnel there were also called upon periodically to assist law enforcement officers at the Trusan Sugut Forest Reserve to curb the extraction of mangrove bark by illegal aliens. He learned that access to the reserve could be had by the Sapi-Nangoh Highway or by the sea route. In Zain's mind, this meant the potentiality of another landing base for aliens with ready dispersal into the interior of Beluran. None of the men manning the police beat base at Sungai-Sungai had heard of an influential man called Sipil.

"Let's also check out with our co-opted members, Nasri, Jamil, and Anton," suggested Sungkiah on their way back to Beluran.

"Yes, of course. They might have heard of him," replied Zain.

Back at their hotel in Beluran, Sungkiah was proven right when Anton recalled the Sipil name being mentioned once in his dealings, but it was one Azmi Sipil, who had a reputation of having a large workforce of illegal immigrants under his care.

"By the way, what is the full name of the Tawau assemblyman?" asked a suddenly curious Zain, turning to Sungkiah.

"Let me check with ACP Rosmah," replied Sungkiah, reaching for her phone. The answer was immediately forthcoming. "Well, I'll be damned! The only assemblyman with the name Adnan is one Datuk Adnan Sipil. I wonder now whether Adnan and Azmi are brothers and partners also in crime."

"Adnan, I suspect, keeps himself in the shadows, and Azmi is his trustworthy operative agent," opined Samy.

"Good. We can now feed Bukit Aman with all the information in our hands. We shall let them nail the Sipil brothers," remarked Zain.

"If we can tie either or both of them with helping Saadam, that piece of evidence alone should be enough to get them a life sentence," ventured Kamal.

"Yes, I suppose Adnan could have financed Saadam's activities. Let's interrogate the Bosnian, Imran, and Haji Jalah, who had dealings with Saadam. Their trials are still pending, and I believe they are still in Sandakan Prison," suggested Zain.

The interrogation that followed drew a blank with Imran, but Haji Jalah gave them the break they were looking for. He recalled being asked to cash an uncrossed personal cheque for thirty thousand ringgits bearing Adnan Sipil's name. The cheque, he claimed, was brought over to Saadam by someone in an army car.

CHAPTER 21

*T*he raiders that landed in Pulau Jambongan finally made their way to the Trusan-Sugut Forest Reserve along riverine routes aided by local guides. They were joined there by other militants who had sneaked in from Kudat and Kota Kinabalu. A terror cell was created within five weeks. Smuggled firearms from Tawau and elsewhere arrived there every week by road, as well as by boat. It soon became a fortified base for the insurgents.

The Sapi-Nangoh Highway also provided for the ease of movement of the insurgents into villages along the road and in the interior areas of Beluran. Prospecting for recruits began in earnest. Heading the terrorist camp was Faizal Shahabuddin, high on the wanted list of terrorists in the Philippines.

The abysmal ignorance of their presence in Sabah by SCSC was a matter of some wonder. Even Zain had assumed that the insurgents were presently lying low and that there were no fresh arrivals. It was again the CIA team of Jack and Jim that woke them up from their slumber.

Giving Zain a call on their way down from Kudat, Jim casually asked, "I see heavy military convoys on the road from Kota Marudu heading towards Sandakan. We just overtook them at Pitas. What gives?"

Zain was surprised. "Nothing of an emergency, as far as I have heard. Perhaps it's their regular troop movement to and fro."

"Jack has been picking out some worrying satellite images of movements in the jungle stretch around Sungai-Sungai, particularly over the last couple of weeks. Thought we should let you know."

"Oh? That's interesting. Are you on your way to Sandakan? We could meet up once you get here at the Four Points Sheraton."

"No problem, but it looks like it will take an eternity to get there. You can't imagine the potholes on the road, and the hogging of the two-lane road by the slow-moving palm oil tankers. The slow-paced road construction is also a nuisance. Hopefully, once we hit the highway, we can breathe a little easier."

It took the CIA agents over five hours to get to Sandakan. Meeting up with Zain, they heard the news.

"A car laden with some 50 kg of RDX explosives driving in the opposite direction, about 10 kilometres towards Pitas, struck the military convoy that was carrying some few hundred soldiers and paramilitary personnel. A suicide bomber was at the wheel of the car. As the vehicles were closely behind one other while negotiating the climb on the road, the damage was extensive, and spread across a wide area. The video shots of the incident appearing on television were gruesome to watch, with body parts and vehicle fragments littered all over the place. At least 30 paramilitary personnel and a dozen or more soldiers were killed and many wounded in the attack. Both BIFF and ISIS have claimed credit for the dastardly attack. Wide stretches of the road and the highway have now been closed to all civilian traffic and a curfew has been imposed on several neighbouring districts."

"Holy crap!" exclaimed Jack. "This can only mean that the insurgents have regrouped to organize this major attack."

"Yes, the worst since the insurgency began. But it also shows that their operational base could not be far from Golong, where we had already busted one of their cells," said Zain.

"I see. OK. Let's show you our satellite surveillance images. The ones taken at night are particularly noteworthy. The activity is mostly around Sungai-Sungai, which you will notice has excellent access to riverine and road transport. They may have established one or more cells in the surrounding jungle areas here. What do you think?"

"I agree. I have been in that area lately and suspect that the Trusan-Sugut Forest Reserve has the potential to serve as one of such strongholds. I have checked its location on the map. The Reserve can be accessed through the Sapi-Nangoh Highway and then through an oil palm estate road, and also by boat from the coast along the river Sungai Sugut."

"Can we get the coordinates of those likely spots indicated on your satellite images?" asked Azlan. "We can then send the drones over these suspect areas to get more focussed pictures."

"Hmm, let me see. Yup, there are three standout spots. Let me work their coordinates now," replied Jack.

Zain turned to look at his pahlawans. Their faces reflected the thought in his mind – *hunt the bastards down.*

A long silence followed, with each one busy with his thoughts. Zain then broke the silence. "I shall get the commander of SCSC, Datuk Johari, to get the drones into action, and inform him of our intent to flush out the insurgents."

"Let's meet later this evening to discuss this together with Brigadier General Othman at the Sandakan Police HQ," came the reply from Datuk Johari to Zain's phone call. He had flown up from Lahad Datu immediately upon receiving the news of the bomb blast.

The CIA duo then took their leave, carrying with them profound thanks from Zain and his pahlawans for their critical intelligence help.

At the meeting at the Sandakan Police HQ, it was resolved that the drones would take to the air the first thing the following morning, and once identification of the target was confirmed, a joint commando raid would be mounted at dusk. The same army team that had cooperated with Zain and his pahlawans at the Kabili-Sepilok Nature Resort was assigned to the task.

As anticipated, the drone pictures hinted strongly of a hideout encompassing three buildings deep inside the Trusan-Sugut FR. The place was about 1.5 kilometres away from the outer reaches of either Sungai Sugut or the estate roads.

It was decided that the army team would take the riverine route from the coast, while Zain and his pahlawans would use the land approach to the site. The time for the assault was set at 3.00 a.m. Both teams were well-equipped for the attack, with a battery of weapons that included a mix of carbines and assault rifles, disposable grenade launchers, mortars, sniper rifles, and night-vision equipment.

They found that the buildings were arranged in a triangular format. A recce showed that each of the buildings had a back exit. The two teams broke up into six units to cover the front and back entrances of the three buildings before they launched the attack. At precisely 3.00 a.m., the signal to fire was given. The buildings were heavily pounded at their front ends with grenades and mortars, setting them all ablaze. Carbines and sniper rifles then sprang into action, catching all the fleeing inmates from the buildings. Only a few with rifles above their heads were spared the fury of shots from the pahlawans and the army personnel, still nurturing their anger at the suicide bombing.

The enemy was caught completely by surprise by the suddenness of the attack and was unable to offer any defensive or retaliatory action using the arsenal of weapons they possessed in their buildings. There was aimless machine gun fire only from one of the buildings, but this could not be sustained.

The two teams then charged into the buildings, which had many dead bodies and severely wounded men. The wounded and those that surrendered were brought to the centre point of the triangular space shared by the buildings. Counted among the severely wounded was their leader, Faizal Shahabuddin.

Save for suffering from some graze gunshot wounds, Zainal and his team encountered no major casualties. Similarly, for members of the army team.

Zain then made a quick phone call. Three military trucks ordered to be in-waiting on the Sapi-Nangoh Highway, just outside the estate entrance, responded promptly to the phone call, and made their way to the end of the estate road previously marked out to them. The wounded and dead militants were taken immediately to a hospital, with a portion of the army team accompanying them in escort in two of the trucks. The rest, including Zain and his pahlawans, boarded the third truck to the police HQ at Sandakan. It was almost 7.00 a.m. when they arrived. There were refreshments already waiting for them, along with the message of a meeting specially scheduled by Datuk Johari for their participation at 8.00 a.m.

Zain then made a quick phone call. Three military trucks ordered to be in-waiting on the Sapi-Nangoh Highway, just outside the estate entrance, responded promptly to the phone call, and made their way to the end of the estate road previously marked out to them. The wounded and dead militants were taken immediately to a hospital, with a portion of the army team accompanying them in escort in two of the trucks. The rest, including Zain and his pahlawans, boarded the third truck to the police HQ at Sandakan. It was almost 7.00 a.m. when they arrived. There were refreshments already waiting for them, along with the message of a meeting specially scheduled by Datuk Johari for their participation at 8.00 a.m.

The meeting was jubilant. Both Datuk Johari and General Othman had only words of praise for Zainal and his pahlawans for bringing to book the terrorists responsible for the heinous suicide bombings that had claimed the lives of the country's soldiers. The army team also came in for some praise for their highly supportive role in the mission. At that point, ASP Arshad joined them; he also offered his congratulations to both teams.

Zain, in his response, thanked all of them, including the army team, for their understanding and support, *"without which nothing could have been so speedily achieved."* He then turned to a pensive mood in expressing the hope that the roundup of the militants, their sympathisers, and supporters, illegal immigrants, and the corrupt law officers would take place with immediate effect. This included also bringing to book errant firms and banks indulging in money laundering, widely held to be the prime source of operational funds for the militants.

He went on next to highlight some weaknesses he and his team saw in CASH, and the need for intensified patrols along the coast, particularly the stretch from the Turtle Islands to Pulau Jambongan.

"And, if I may add one more observation," chipped in Sungkiah. All eyes turned towards her. "We cannot always be in a reactive mode; we need to be proactive, and that means putting more agents in the field to gather intelligence about sleeper cells. The suicide bombing on our military convoy that we witnessed the other day could probably have been avoided if that had been the case."

"We recognize the need, but I'm afraid it takes a lot of manpower for that. Without sufficient approbation from the Ministries of Home Affairs & Defence, this might not come to pass," observed Arshad, registering frustration on his face.

Zain, then leaning forward on the table, said in a measured voice, "There's yet one other vulnerable area that we haven't brought to your attention, and that is Pulau Sebatik. There are terror training cells in the making just across the border on the Indonesian side that need to be quickly skittled by drone-assisted assaults conducted jointly by Malaysian and Indonesian border patrols. I cannot also overemphasise our need to deploy more drones both inland and along the coast for strengthening our surveillance."

He paused to see both General Othman and Datuk Johari nodding their heads in agreement, before continuing.

"We have already stumbled onto one terror cell in Pulau Sebatik by tailing some militants with their recruits. JAD has got a foothold on the Indonesian part of the island. We suspect there might be growing collusion between them and the Bangsamoro Group from Mindanao in bringing turmoil to Sabah. Their sole aim here is to establish an Islamic State copying the example of Iraq and Syria while not entirely decrying the return of a Sulu sultanate to the state.

"We have also heard a rumour from our adventitious contact with two CIA agents in Sabah that Saadam's assistant from Afghanistan is on his way here via Kalimantan. So far, we have not been able to confirm the rumour, but if he is, indeed, in this part of the world, I imagine he would not find a better sanctuary than the one on Pulau Sebatik to launch his evil plans. I must also acknowledge the role of the CIA agents in alerting us to the unusual movements their satellite imagery had captured in the jungle areas around Sungai-Sungai. We wouldn't have requested the confirmatory drone surveillance were it not for that critical bit of intelligence."

"It's truly astounding what you have all achieved. We shall take note of your observations. We can't thank you enough," replied Datuk Johari.

"Same here. You have certainly put us on our toes," added General Othman.

"So, will you be heading back to Kuala Lumpur soon?" asked Arshad.

"Yes, I guess so. But we have one bit of unfinished business. That is to bust the terror cell we had previously identified in Pulau Sebatik and bring back the falsely recruited lads from Kampung Kerinchi who are being indoctrinated against their will to become terrorists. We owe it to the ketua kampung of the village. Perhaps this can be accomplished again jointly with SCSC."

"Once that is done?"

"Once that is done, I guess we have to report to MinDef and General Ghazali on the outcome of our undercover mission here. For all you know, there is the possibility our team may still be on standby for a while longer before being disbanded."

"You and your pahlawans will always find a welcome here," said General Othman, standing up, along with Datuk Johari and Arshad, to shake their hands individually.

The End

Made in the USA
Monee, IL
09 October 2022